Yonder

ALSO BY
Ali Standish

Ali Standish

Yonder

HARPER
An imprint of HarperCollinsPublishers

Library of Congress Control Number: 2021949305
ISBN 978-0-06-298568-2

Typography by Joel Tippie and Laura Mock
22 23 24 25 26   SB   10 9 8 7 6 5 4 3 2 1

First Edition

For Luka,
who teaches me to be brave

The land of our better selves
is most surely reached by walking.

—Inscription at Beacon Heights,
mile 305.1, Blue Ridge Parkway
Author Unknown

Prologue

Prologue

Every hero has a story.

Stories, I've learned, are a bit like hearts. We've all got one inside us, locked away just out of sight.

But just because you know there's a heart beating in the chest of the person standing right beside you doesn't mean you can hear it. Mostly, you never do.

Stories are the same way. Told in whispers, as often as not. So you have to listen close to hear them.

I think you have to listen especially close when it comes to heroes.

We all want to *see* heroes. To pat them on the back and shake their hands and tell them what a swell job they've done and how thankful we are.

We want them to be brave, but we don't want to hear what that bravery has cost them. We don't want to know that underneath all that bravery is fear, deep and cold as the Watauga River after the first spring thaw. We don't want to hear their stories. Not their true stories, anyway.

We'd rather tell stories of our own.

It was that way when the soldiers went off to war and when they came home. And it was that way with Jack, too.

The first time I took much notice of Jack Bailey was about the same time lots of folks in Foggy Gap did. It was the summer of 1940, and I was ten years old. It had been raining for three days straight. A hurricane blowing in off the coast had thrown a surprise left hook worthy of a champion prize fighter and come barreling toward Appalachia.

The rain was still pouring down, and the water was ankle-high in some of the streets as we waded to church on Sunday morning.

The whole congregation sat soggy and shivering as Pastor Douglass shouted over the storm. He gave an especially heated sermon that morning, like he thought maybe the fire in his voice could drive the damp cold from our pews. It was as he banged his fist against the pulpit to emphasize the power of the Lord's will that the church groaned and seemed to give a great lurch, like a spooked horse.

Before Pastor Douglass could say another word, half the congregation was running for the doors to see what was going on. Thankfully, my family's normal pew was toward the back, which meant I was able to squirm through the adults gathering on the church steps to see what they were staring at.

The Watauga had burst its banks, and the dirt road that separated the river from the church had now completely disappeared under swiftly flowing water, the color of Daddy's morning coffee. In fact, half the church steps were already underwater.

My best friend, Lou, shoved in next to me. "Look, Danny!" she cried out gleefully as she gripped my arm. "There goes Mr. Maynard's car!"

Mrs. Maguire quickly clapped a white-gloved hand over Lou's mouth, but by then the rest of us had already spotted the brand-new Oldsmobile being carried away by the water. From behind me, I heard a man who could have only been Mr. Maynard yell something that certainly had never been uttered on those church steps before. Quick as a flash, Lou's mother's hands moved from Lou's mouth to her ears.

Then someone else cried out. People began to point to an object floating toward us.

As it drew closer, I saw it wasn't one object but two. And then that they weren't objects at all but two little girls. The Coombs twins, who had stayed home from church that morning on account of having the chicken pox, were floating side by side in the water, flailing and sputtering for breath.

"They'll drown!" shouted Mrs. Updike as the twins neared. "Somebody do something!"

There was a moment's pause when we all searched ourselves for the courage to jump in, each one of us finding instead an excuse not to.

Then, from somewhere to my left, I heard a familiar voice—one that never failed to make me flinch.

"My daddy can do it," Bruce Pittman crowed. "He's the best swimmer in town."

And with that, all eyes turned from the twins to the Pittmans. Mr. Pittman stood behind Bruce. His face went sallow, his knuckles turning white on his son's shoulders. His features were pinched like he had just stepped in a steaming pile of horse manure.

Mr. Pittman's eyes flickered to the bobbing heads in the swift, churning water. He licked his lips.

"They're going under!" squealed Mrs. Maguire as the two tiny heads disappeared beneath the water.

Mr. Pittman opened his mouth to say something, but we never found out what it was. An elbow jutted into my ribs as people were pushed aside. Then, the flash of someone diving into the water. He was tall but his shoulders narrow. A boy who wasn't quite yet a man.

For a long moment, he didn't reappear, and I thought

whoever the boy was, he might have drowned.

"Who was that?" I heard Mama ask Daddy.

"I think it's John Bailey's boy," Daddy replied. "Jack, isn't it?

The name began to ripple through the crowd. I only knew Jack Bailey from a distance then, as a boy three years ahead of me in school who wore the same ratty clothes every day.

Behind us all, Pastor Douglass began to pray loudly. "Our Holy Father, maker of heaven and earth—"

But no one else joined in. We were too busy watching as Jack Bailey suddenly reappeared, hoisting an arm beneath the shoulders of each tiny twin. Then he began to swim toward a river birch that had been felled by the flood (and which was likely what had shaken the church) but whose roots still held fast. If he could get to the tree and lift the girls onto it, they would be able to shimmy along the trunk all the way to where its upper branches rested on dry land.

At first, it looked like they weren't going to make it. The current wanted to sweep them forward, not allow them a sideways detour. But then Jack seemed to find some strength he must have been saving up and began to kick, harder and harder, and the people on the steps began to shout.

"You can do it, son!"

"Little faster now, that's it!"

Then he had reached the birch tree, which gave him enough protection from the current to lift the Coombs twins one at a time onto the trunk. The girls coughed up river water as Jack hoisted himself up after them.

We watched as he gently pushed them to start scooting their way along the trunk toward dry land.

By that time, a few men had run through the church's back door and along the hillside graveyard that still sat above the rising water, where the top of the tree had landed. As soon as the twins were near enough, two of the men reached through the boughs to lift each of them off. Behind them, Jack jumped down.

The moment they were all on dry land, everyone began to clap and cheer. Some of the women held their handkerchiefs to their noses or eyes, though the handkerchiefs must already have been soaked from the rain. Mr. Maynard looked close to tears, too, though I thought it was more likely he was misty-eyed over his car than out of relief for the twins.

Only Mr. Pittman looked more unhappy. Bruce, too, was scowling, his cheeks flushed. I elbowed Lou and nodded over at him. She snorted in appreciation.

I turned my gaze back toward Jack. I thought he might wave or cheer or grin, the way a boy might if he'd hit a home run or won a round of capture the flag. Instead, he tilted his chin toward the sky and closed his eyes against the rain. Like that water might baptize him anew, even though he'd already been washed clean by the river. Like it was him who had needed saving that day instead of the Coombs twins.

No one else saw the rawboned boy point his face skyward. They were too busy clutching each other and laughing in relief, already telling one another the story, as if we hadn't all just seen it for ourselves.

Daddy put Jack on the front page the next day. LOCAL HERO SAVES TODDLER TWINS FROM DROWNING DEATH, read the headline.

And from then on, that's what Jack Bailey was. Not a boy. A hero.

We argued over the specifics. How long Jack went under the water (some people swore he'd been down there a full two minutes). How much those twins must have weighed soaking wet. Whether he'd found the strength from within or whether it was given to him by the Lord, whom Pastor Douglass had called down to help not a moment too soon.

But we all agreed on the main thing. Jack Bailey was a hero.

We didn't stop to wonder what that made us.

So that was the story we told about Jack. The story that followed him for years, like a faithful old dog. But that was not *Jack's* story.

Despite everything that would happen between us, I'm not sure I ever knew his story.

I think he tried, once, to tell me. It was months after Jack had come to stay with us, after we'd started doing the paper route together. After I'd come to think of him as my friend. We were lying on our backs on the river dock, basking in the sun. Summer was just spreading its bright wings over Foggy Gap.

That was the day he'd told me about Yonder.

Maybe if I had been listening more closely, I would have understood what he was trying to say.

Maybe then when he went missing, I would have known that Officer Sawyer was right. It would have been better not to look for him at all.

But I was too busy trying to be a detective, searching for clues. Like Nancy Drew, who always solved the case in the books Lou gave me to read (in secret—if Bruce Pittman caught me reading a book about a girl, he'd have hated me worse than he already did).

I wish now I had tried as hard to be a good friend as I tried to be the hero of the story. Maybe then I could have been both.

But there was so much I didn't understand then. About Jack, about our own small town, and the great wide world. About war. And about my place in all of it.

I didn't yet understand that every hero has a story.

But not every story has a hero.

Even now, after all this time, I'm still trying to figure out which one this is.

A hero's story. Or a story without a hero.

1

June 1943
FRIDAY

Just before Jack disappeared, it had been stifling hot in Foggy Gap. That was rare. Usually even when the temperatures climbed to swimming-hole weather, a breeze would float down off the mountains, the same way Mama blew on my brow when I was feverish.

But that June, we'd have had better luck waiting for a breeze blowing in from the sea. Of course, though three whole years had passed since the Great Flood of 1940, none of us would ever wish for a sea breeze again. The flood might have ultimately spared the Coombs twins, but it had taken a good deal more from Foggy Gap than just Mr. Maynard's car.

When I woke up on Friday morning, I found the

rainstorm from the night before had broken the heat. I thrust my window open higher and emptied the rain-water from the bucket I had set out underneath where the roof leaked. It had been a hard rain, all right. The bucket was nearly full. But now the dawn was turning pink, last night's storm already forgotten.

Mama wasn't awake yet when I got to the kitchen. That wasn't so unusual these days. Not since she'd gotten bigger around the middle. The baby, she said, made her awfully tired.

I didn't like thinking too much about the baby, even if Granny Mabel called it a "miracle child" in her letters (because in all the nearly thirteen years since I'd been born, Mama had never had another). I would have plenty of time to think about the baby once it arrived. Then we'd see about all that miracle business.

I brought in the morning's milk from our front stoop and poured some over a bowl of cornflakes. I started to shake a teaspoon of sugar over them, but as I picked up the jar, I could feel that it was almost empty. We had no more stamps for sugar left in our ration book that month, so I put the jar back.

Sugar was a small sacrifice, as sacrifices went in those days.

It was like the signs in the shop windows in town said. *Rationing means a fair share for all of us!*

Feeling satisfied with this minor act of patriotism, I wolfed down the soggy cereal, drained the milk from the bowl, and headed for the door. Outside, warblers and wrens were already filling the pine boughs with song. Ripening tomatoes hung on the vines in the victory garden Mrs. Musgrave had helped Mama and me plant after Daddy left for the war.

We lived in a two-story cedar house with a driveway and a porch at the end of a street of other two-story cedar houses with driveways and porches. They had all been built before the Great Depression, and you could tell by looking at them how the families inside had fared in those years.

("First we had the Great War," Lou said to me once, back when we were still friends. "Then the Great Depression. And then the Great Flood. I wish Greatness would just leave us be for once." And I couldn't help thinking that she had a point.)

I inhaled the smell of bacon and rising biscuits as I biked past the familiar houses toward town. I kept time as I climbed up the hill toward the newspaper office, trying to see if I could beat my personal best of forty-seven seconds. The burn in my calves made me proud as I whizzed easily past Dinwiddie's General Store and the Skyline Diner. The sun was just starting to break over the mountains like an egg cracked into a frying pan.

Mornings like that, it was easy to forget about the war, even though the papers I delivered every day were full of it. Even though victory gardens just like ours had sprouted up in lots of other lawns, and service flags hung from the windows of many of the houses on my route. We had a service flag in our front window, too, with one blue star stitched on it. That star was a reminder of Daddy, who was somewhere overseas fighting his share of the war.

His last letter had come only days ago and had assured us that he was doing just fine, though the food was terrible. I don't know what he wrote after that, because the censors had blacked out his words. Even when I tried to make a rubbing of his letter on another sheet of paper, I couldn't make anything out. We weren't allowed to know anything about where Daddy was or what he was doing.

I pulled up in front of the *Herald* office just as the first beads of sweat were appearing on my forehead. I looked for Jack's bike, but it was nowhere to be seen. That was unusual, because Jack nearly always got to the office before I did. A bell chimed as the door opened and Mr. Maynard came trundling out, chest puffed up like he was looking for a fight (which he usually was).

"Morning, Mr. Maynard."

He tipped his hat at me before glancing down at his

watch. "Little late, aren't we?"

"Yessir."

If I was late, that meant Jack was even later.

"Your mama going to be in this morning?"

"Yessir."

"Good," he said, without sounding like he meant it. He wiped the sweat from his forehead, which was quite large on account of his receding hairline, before putting his hat back on. "We have some things to talk about. Better get on your way. The news won't keep, will it?"

I suppressed a yawn. "No, sir."

Mr. Maynard owned all the papers in our corner of the mountains, including the *Hilltop Herald*. Until Daddy had enlisted that January, he had been editor of the *Herald*. When he left, he had convinced Mr. Maynard to let Mama take his place. She'd been to college to study English literature after all, and it's not like there was a line of men waiting to fill Daddy's shoes. Women were doing all sorts of jobs that had belonged to men before.

Mr. Maynard had reluctantly agreed but had taken to buzzing around the office like a great big carpenter bee. Determined to make trouble wherever he could. He nearly turned purple when Mama told him about the baby, but she insisted she could keep doing the job, and so she had.

Just outside the office, the day's papers had been tied into bundles. Jack and I delivered them to all the businesses and houses in town, while Billy Updike drove the rest out to the folks who lived down in the hollers and out on the farms, where red barns dotted the green hills like ladybugs crawling all over a summer garden.

Billy's share of papers was gone, but the stacks that belonged to Jack and me were both still waiting.

Jack and I had been delivering the papers together for a year and a half. Each morning, we took our time biking together all the way down Poplar Street, where most of the shops and businesses were, before going our separate ways. The time we spent biking beside each other, joking and swapping stories, was my favorite part of the day. In those quiet early-morning moments, it felt like the whole town belonged only to us. And in all those months, he'd been late only once or twice.

I suspected he didn't want to hang around home a minute longer than he needed to.

Most days, I stuck some breakfast leftovers into my saddlebags for him, but that morning I'd forgotten. Which was just as well, since there was still no trace of him. If people didn't get their papers on time, they'd complain, and my pay would be docked.

I loaded my share of papers into my saddlebags,

glancing at the front page as I did. There was the weekly list of license plates belonging to drivers who had been caught breaking the new thirty-five-mile-per-hour speed limit imposed to help save fuel, and a stern reminder that the war effort needed gasoline more than we did. An advertisement for the feed store in Whistling Hill, the next town over. A piece on the coal miner strikes. Nothing much of interest.

When I'd loaded all my papers and there was still no sign of Jack, I decided I couldn't wait any longer. So I crammed the rest of the papers into my saddlebags and set off.

"You owe me, Jack Bailey," I grumbled under my breath. "And you had better have one good excuse."

2

Downtown only stretched a few blocks, from the filling station on one end to town hall on the other. In between, there was the bank, an insurance office, the barbershop, Dr. Penny's office, the library, the general store, the diner, and a few other buildings made from stone or brick, none of them taller than two stories. This early, there were hardly any cars parked outside the businesses—and no horses with carts either.

When I was done with Poplar Street, I delivered to the houses closest to town, most of them modest wooden homes with soft mossy roofs and tidy porches. The families without service banners had American flags that flapped in the breeze or hung from the windows. Forest grew up behind the houses so they looked like pretty pictures painted on a green canvas.

Some homes, like Dylan Price's, had a tree out front, too. As I threw the Prices' paper, I saw that all the curtains were drawn in their house, though we hadn't had a blackout drill in some time. The star that hung on their banner wasn't blue like ours was. It was gold.

Gold meant that somebody wouldn't be returning from the war.

I had been sitting right next to Dylan when Mr. Bunch, our principal, had called him out of class two weeks before so his mother could tell him the news. But I don't think she needed to. I think he knew the moment Mr. Bunch called his name that his father had died. Those of us who had someone fighting were half expecting it all the time.

I was suddenly in a hurry to get away from the Price house, so I nearly missed the bottle cap someone had tossed on the side of the road and had to circle back to pick it up. Into my pocket it went, to be added to my scrap-metal collection later.

As I crossed the bridge that took me over the Watauga—still roaring from last night's storm—my mind wandered back to Jack. I kept thinking he might appear behind me at any moment. What could have kept him?

I supposed he could be sick, but I'd never known him to catch so much as a cold. And he had been fine the day before. Besides, Jack needed the money too much to stay home.

His father, Mr. Bailey, did lots of work—curing tobacco, sweating in the paper mill over in Whistling Hill, even delivering coal. He just never did it for long before he became too disagreeable for the work, or the work became too disagreeable to him. So I knew the money Jack earned on the paper route wasn't just pocket money.

Once I had delivered papers to all the houses in town, I widened my route to include the closest farms, where the day had long since started. On the far side of the river was the Musgraves' place, the house and barn separated from the road by a gnarled old apple orchard. The Musgraves had been gone for a few months by then, but I still hadn't gotten used to the silence as I passed by their drive. The sound of Mrs. Musgrave singing often used to drift down from the farmhouse or the barn, where she went about her morning routine. I liked to stop a minute to listen to her voice, clear and sure as a mountain creek that knows each coming bend and tumble.

Sometimes her son, Jordan, would be waiting at the bottom of the drive for me. I would see him standing on tiptoe as I rode around the bend in the road, craning his neck to see me coming. He cradled the paper to his chest when I handed it down to him, always remembering to murmur a shy *thank you* before he tore off back to the house. I had never seen a little kid so excited about the paper before, and I didn't understand why he cared so much about it until Mama explained what had happened with the librarian, Mrs. Ballentine.

As I gazed up at the house, the memory turned me suddenly sullen, like a cherry I had bitten into expecting it to be sweet, only to find it sour on my tongue. The Musgraves' house was empty now, their land run by someone Mr. Pittman had hired after he bought their farm.

I turned away and kept riding. My very last paper was for the Widow Wagner, who lived at the top of a steep hill on the road that led west out of town. Really, Billy Updike should have delivered her paper in his truck, since he drove right by it on his route. But he refused to because she was a German.

When it came to it, I didn't much like the idea of delivering her paper, either. Partially because the hill was so steep, and partially because the widow gave me the creeps. That's why I had always let Jack deliver there.

The house itself was pretty. It was blue with pink gingerbread trim all along the eaves. The Widow Wagner had lived there since before I was born—and been a widow at least that long, too—but I knew she and her husband had moved from Germany after the First World War.

For as long as I could remember, the widow had kept herself to herself. When we were younger, we all used to gather around after Sunday school to tell stories about her. Some kids said she was a witch. A *real* witch. Maybe even the one from that old fairy tale "Hansel and Gretel." She was German, wasn't she, and she had just the right kind of house.

More recently, Bruce Pittman had assured us that the Widow Wagner was hiding other Germans who had escaped from a nearby prisoner-of-war camp. He said they were holed up in there, probably plotting an attack on our town while she made them sauerkraut by the bucketload.

Maybe we believed Bruce or maybe we just pretended. We were all as afraid of him as we were of the widow. But by now it hardly mattered. Just like we had all long agreed that Jack was a hero, so, too, did we understand that the widow was a villain.

But Mama said she was a paying customer, and she would get what she paid for, like anyone else. For his part, Jack never complained about the hill or the house. He had never let some old stories scare him, so neither would I now.

I was nearly thirteen, after all. Far too old to be scared by the widow.

I was out of breath by the time I reached the top of the hill and dug into my saddlebags to pull out one last paper. I threw it onto the brick path that led up to the porch.

As if to prove to myself that I really wasn't afraid, I took a good long look at the house. I straightened my shoulders at the stained glass above the front door and narrowed my eyes at the heavy curtains drawn against the upstairs windows. Just in case anyone was watching.

Even as I thought it, I saw a flicker of motion and just caught the outline of someone in the second-story window before the curtain fell back into place.

A shiver crawled down my neck like a spider. Visions of hulking, hungry Germans invaded my mind.

The next moment, I was flying down the hill toward school, away from the widow's house and its secrets.

3

Depending on the season, and who you were walking past, you could smell all sorts of things in Mrs. Pattershaw's classroom. There was always the sharp whiff of pencil shavings but also the scent of wet wool or curing tobacco, cooked apples or fresh pine sap. Unfortunately, there was usually even fresher pig slop in the mix, too.

I didn't have time to stop and smell the slop that morning, though. When I shoved myself through the classroom door, still panting from running up the stairs, Mrs. Pattershaw didn't waste a moment.

"You're late, Danny," she said, tucking her chin to her chest, frowning at me over the frame of her glasses.

"Detention at lunch. Take your seat now, please."

"Yes, ma'am," I muttered. I knew better than to try to plead my case. If I stayed quiet now, she might have mercy on me and let me have the last ten minutes of the lunch period off. Then I could sneak down to the high school corridor and see if Jack was there.

I kept my head bowed as I trudged toward my desk, which was lucky because I saw Bruce's foot jut out just as I was about to walk by. I stopped short.

Bruce had trouble written all over his face, from his orange freckles to the ugly little scar on his chin to the mean shine of his eye. Though his father owned half the farms around town, Bruce always looked scrubbed clean, and I suspected he'd never so much as held a hoe.

He winked when he caught me looking at him. "Just kidding," he mouthed, sliding his foot back under his desk.

I forced a smile, trying to pretend I was in on the joke. But I knew what it really was.

A reminder.

Logan Abbot, Bruce's right-hand man, snorted from the next desk over.

I supposed I should just be grateful they hadn't seen the way I'd fled from the Widow Wagner's house that morning. It would have been another arrow for Bruce to add to the quiverful he reserved just for me. *Awww, is little Danny scared? Need a shoulder to cry on?*

From the corner of my eye, I could sense Lou staring. Ducking into my seat, I pulled out my spelling book. Dylan Price sat in the seat next to mine, looking small and pale as he stared out the window, lost in his own thoughts. I knew Mrs. Pattershaw wouldn't scold him for it. Who could blame him?

I watched the morning drag by on the clock above the chalkboard, the second hand moving so idly I thought it might simply give up ticking at all. When lunch finally arrived, I watched my classmates file out, some of them heading for the cafeteria while the lucky ones headed for home and a hot meal.

When Lou and I were still friends, I used to go home with her sometimes. Mrs. Maguire always poured her butter into molds shaped like chickens or pigs. Lou and I fought over who got to chop the head off. But that was before everything changed for the Maguire family, and then changed between me and Lou. Now, even Lou didn't go home much anymore.

For detention, I had to write a paragraph on the chalkboard about why it was wrong to be late and then diagram each of the sentences. Mrs. Pattershaw sat grading papers at her desk and eating her sandwich, occasionally flicking her eyes toward me and offering a correction. "*Tardy* is an adjective, Danny. Not an adverb."

When I was done, she examined my work. "Full marks for sentence structure," she said. "But what are we going to do about your penmanship?"

Mrs. Pattershaw had a stern voice. But as teachers went, I thought she was all right. She almost never slapped us on the wrist with her ruler.

"Sorry, Mrs. Pattershaw."

"Never mind. That's enough for today. Go now and you might just have time to eat some lunch."

I didn't need to be told twice.

In Foggy Gap, kids went to school in their churches until fifth grade. Then they got to come to the real school, which was a three-story granite building with a gymnasium, a baseball diamond, and a cafeteria. Fifth and sixth graders took classes on the third floor, seventh and eighth on the second floor, and high schoolers on the first.

As a seventh grader, I was supposed to stay on the second floor, so I was relieved to find the first floor halls empty when I got there.

I wasn't sure which class Jack had now, but I knew it wouldn't be math. He had math class last in the day, and Mr. Bunch nearly always made him stay after school to do extra work.

It was no secret that Jack and school got along about as well as a farm dog and a barn cat. It wasn't that he was dim-witted, though some people—Mr. Bunch included—seemed to think so. It was just that letters and figures didn't make sense to him the same way other things did. He could read a coming snow on the wind or count out the loops in a spider hitch knot better than anyone I knew.

Mr. Bailey would rather Jack dropped out so he could spend more time hunting for food, or finding a way to bring in extra money. And plenty of kids did miss school sometimes to do just that, or to help out on their family's farms, especially during harvests. But it seemed like every time Mr. Bailey tried to make Jack stay home, Mr. Rowlands—the town's truant officer, who was in charge of keeping all the local kids in school—would show up and march him straight back to class.

Still, Jack would be sixteen next week. Too old for Mr. Rowlands to be dealing with any longer. And what would happen then?

I peeked into the windows of all the classes except Mr. Bunch's. My face flushed when some of the older students glanced up, but there was no sign of Jack.

There was nothing unusual about the way he looked. He was neither tall nor short, and had sandy brown hair that he clearly cut himself, teeth crowded into irregular rows, and a narrow, clear-eyed face tanned from long hours in the sun. Even so, Jack had a way of standing out in a crowd. Especially now, when so many of the older boys had already enlisted and gone off to fight.

I made it to Mrs. Pattershaw's classroom as the last students filed back in from lunch, but I couldn't concentrate on lessons that afternoon. All kinds of possibilities were spinning out in my mind, none of them good.

I was still thinking about Jack's upcoming birthday, and all those other missing boys in the classrooms downstairs. Sixteen was old enough to do a lot of things. It was old enough to drop out of school, but it was also old enough to enlist to fight in the war with a parent's permission.

But surely Mr. Bailey would never allow Jack to enlist when he could be more useful at home?

I was so deep in my thoughts that the afternoon bell caught me by surprise. I felt lucky that Mrs. Pattershaw hadn't noticed how distracted I had been. She might give Dylan a free pass on account of his father, but I knew I wouldn't get the same treatment.

"Remember, everyone, just a few days left to gather your scrap metal," she called out. "There might only be one winner, but I expect every one of you to do your part for your country."

My heart lifted a bit at that. I had been scrounging around our house and the town every chance I got for bits of scrap metal that the military would melt down and use to build tanks and bullets and things. Things that could win us the war. The kid who collected the most in each grade would be honored in a special ceremony at the end of the year. I had been dreaming for weeks of winning.

As I packed up my things to go, Mrs. Pattershaw called out my name.

"This chalkboard needs washing," she said. "And you're just the man for the job."

Maybe she had noticed my wandering attention after all.

4

"*I know it's nearly* the end of the year," said Mrs. Pattershaw as I finished the chalkboard. "But I don't expect your mother would like to hear that you've not been applying yourself to your schooling. Not in her condition."

"No, ma'am, she wouldn't." I hung my head, trying to look like I felt remorseful.

"Well, go on, then," Mrs. Pattershaw said, a small smile softening her face as she shooed me off. "See you Monday, on your best behavior."

The stairwells were nearly empty, so I took the stairs two at a time. When I stepped out the front doors, I had to stop and screw up my eyes against the dazzling sun. Temporarily blinded, I heard their voices before I saw them.

"Give it back, Bruce!"

"Or what?"

I blinked, my eyes adjusting to the light. At the base of the steps stood Lou, her hands on her hips. Her blond hair was shorn short as a boy's, and she was dressed in overalls that had once belonged to her older brother, George. I wondered if she'd snuck out of the house that way, or if her mama had simply given up on trying. Mrs. Maguire certainly had bigger worries.

Lou had her back to me. She was squared off with Bruce and Logan, who were standing shoulder to shoulder, their legs straddled across their bikes. Bruce, I saw, had a book in his hands. A Nancy Drew book.

My heart sank. The Maguires weren't rich by any stretch. Lou didn't have fancy clothes or many nice things—not that she could have been made to care for them if she did. Her Nancy Drew books were her prized possessions. I knew I should try to help. Lou would have done the same for me, even though we weren't talking anymore.

Instead, I shrank back into the shadows.

Lou sprang forward and took a swipe at the book, but Bruce held it above his head where she couldn't reach. She jumped for it, but he easily passed it off to Logan.

"Just give it back, you knuckleheads," she demanded.

"I'm not sure you want to start with name-calling," said Bruce. But the smile spreading over his face said that he couldn't have been more pleased that she had. "Because I've heard a few going around about your brother."

"How about chicken liver?" said Logan. His voice had changed that past spring, and it was deep as a bullfrog's now. He had the first stubble of a moustache over his lip.

"Wimp."

"Spineless cowa—"

Lou kicked her right leg out, aiming for Bruce's shin. But he was just a hair too fast for her and lifted his leg so her foot sailed through the air and she nearly fell.

"She wants to fight you, Bruce!" guffawed Logan.

"Guess that explains it," Bruce replied, his eyes narrowing. "She wound up with all the fighting genes. Her brother got none."

"You shut your mouths!" Lou yelled. "I *will* fight you! I'll fight you right now!"

"Come and get it," said Bruce, raising the book up high again. As Lou lunged, I realized what was going to happen. Because the same thing had once happened to me.

I couldn't watch. I spun around, darting back into the school building just as a man was hurrying out. I ran smack-dab into his chest, and then I was falling. Backward in air and backward in time.

Before

October 1941

I fell flat on my back, wincing as my head hit the hard-packed dirt. There was a crack of pain where my skull had collided with the ground. But that wasn't the worst of it. I was breathing, but somehow I couldn't catch my breath. My lungs burned. Somewhere close by, I heard laughter.

"Is the little sissy crying?" cackled Logan.

A shadow appeared above me, blocking out the sun. Bruce.

He had been the shadow darkening my life ever since the one and only scout trip Daddy had convinced me to go on.

"Oh no," he jeered. "Is the little baby scared?"

"I think he needs his mommy," Logan said, his voice giddy.

Why had I ever gone on that stupid trip? That trip when we had sat around the campfire, and the older scouts told terrible stories about the things that waited for us in the woods, both living and dead. When Bruce and I were assigned to share a tent. When, after some of the older boys snuck up on us in the middle of the night, pretending to be the very monsters they had warned us about, I had been overcome by terror and begun to cry for Mama.

"Come on, mama's boy," Bruce said, leaning down and smiling at me now. "You know you want to."

It had become a game over the years since the camping trip: Bruce, usually accompanied by Logan, trying to get me to cry again. To prove once more what a sissy I was.

In those days, Lou and I usually rode home from school together, but she'd been out sick with a cold that day, so I was on my own. Bruce and Logan had ridden up behind me as I was biking by the baseball diamond. I had tried to outride them, but it was no use. Logan had grabbed one of my saddlebags and jerked it, sending my bike skidding and me falling to the ground.

Lying there now, I gasped, and a little air trickled back into my body. Cold, but welcome.

"Come on," Bruce coaxed, sounding almost friendly. "Cry. We won't tell."

"No," I croaked.

Even though I could hardly breathe, I mustered enough strength to sit up. As I tried to scramble to my feet, Bruce pulled his fist back in the air, like a snake before it strikes. I threw my hands up in front of my face, waiting for the blow to come.

Instead, I heard a yelp.

When I lowered my hands, I saw someone yanking Bruce by the back of his collar. It was Jack Bailey.

Bruce was bigger than me, but Jack had filled out by then, and he had at least thirty pounds on Bruce. He pulled Bruce away with all the effort it might have taken to grab an unruly puppy by the scruff of its neck.

In another second, Jack had pinned him up roughly against the dugout wall. Logan stood to the side, frozen and slack-jawed.

"You okay?" Jack asked. They were the first words he had ever spoken to me, and it took me a moment to realize who he was talking to.

"Yeah," I said. "Except I can't breathe too good."

"That one probably knocked the wind out of you," he said, nodding to Logan. "Take a few deep breaths and you'll be fine."

His voice was calm and even, like it was the most natural thing in the world to be giving medical advice while pinning Bruce Pittman to a wall.

By then, Bruce's face was scarlet with anger, but his

eyes were wide and skittish. "Get off me!" he growled, trying to shoulder free of Jack's grip and spitting at his feet when he couldn't.

A look flashed through Jack's eyes then, making them hard and bright as diamonds. His jaw went stiff, and for a moment I was sure he was going to punch Bruce, right in the face.

"You—" he started.

But then he stopped. He closed his eyes, and when they opened, the hard look was gone. "I catch you pushing him around again, you'll be sorry, hear?"

Bruce mumbled something I couldn't make out.

"What was that?" Jack asked.

"I said I heard you!" Bruce barked.

"Good," said Jack. "Go on, then."

He relaxed his grip on Bruce, who darted to his bike.

"You know, my daddy says you're nothing but trash. You just wait until he hears about this," said Bruce when he was safely out of Jack's reach. "Then you'll be sorry!"

Jack shrugged indifferently. "Your daddy don't scare me."

Throwing me a last dirty look, Bruce rode off behind Logan, who had jumped at the chance to get a head start.

Jack stared after them until they disappeared into the woods. Then he turned back to me and held out his hand. "I'm Jack," he said. "Jack Bailey."

On the day he had rescued the Coombs twins from the Great Flood, Jack had become the town hero. But the day he rescued me from Bruce was the day he became mine.

5

June 1943

Instantly, hands were reaching for me. Pulling me back up to my feet. It took me a moment to remember where I was. Not by the baseball field but on the front steps of the school. More than a year and a half had passed since Jack had kept Bruce from pummeling me, and this time it wasn't me that Bruce and Logan were hunting. It was Lou.

The pale face pulling me up came into focus. It was Mr. Bunch. Mr. Bunch was Jack's teacher, but he was also the school principal. He'd begun teaching math only after the regular teacher had enlisted.

"Next time, pay more attention to where you're going, Mr. Timmons." His voice dripped with annoyance.

Then he brushed past me. Lou was picking herself up from the ground. Her book was splayed on the grass, like a dead thing. Bruce and Logan were laughing as they mounted their bikes.

"You boys. Stop!" Mr. Bunch demanded. He was a short man with a voice that squeaked like soggy boots, but he was still the principal.

Bruce and Logan turned to face him, with identical expressions of innocent confusion.

"Are you all right?" he asked, approaching Lou. "Did they push you down?"

Lou's hair stuck up at the back. Over her dirt-smudged cheeks, she glared between Bruce, Logan, and Mr. Bunch. Taking her time, she reached down for the book.

"Nope," she said.

"No?" repeated Mr. Bunch. "But I thought I saw—"

"No, sir," said Lou. "I tripped. Ma's always saying I'm as clumsy as a blindfolded badger, with only half as many manners. That's why my deportment grades are so low."

That almost made me smile. And even though Lou was standing right in front of me, I missed her fiercely just then.

Mr. Bunch frowned. He turned to me.

"You saw what happened, didn't you?"

I could feel Lou's eyes on me. Bruce's and Logan's, too.

"No," I mumbled. "I didn't see a thing."

"May we go, sir?" said Bruce, his voice as buttoned up and proper as his Sunday best. "My father needs me for my chores."

Mr. Bunch looked as if he had finally run into a calculation he couldn't solve, trying to decide whether to call Bruce out on his lie, when his father was the most powerful man in town.

Finally, he sighed. "Fine," he said. "Just get on home."

I glanced at Lou. She was brushing *Nancy Drew* off on the leg of her overalls.

"Mr. Timmons," Mr. Bunch said as I tried to slip away. "Wait just a moment. You're always hanging around with Jack Bailey, aren't you?"

"We're friends," I corrected, unhappy with the suggestion that I simply *hung around* Jack, like a pesky mosquito.

"Well, he wasn't in class today," said Mr. Bunch. "Math may not be as interesting to him as fishing, but he missed his final exam. If he doesn't show up tomorrow, tell him our deal is off."

"Oh . . . all right," I mumbled, taken aback. "What deal is that?"

Mr. Bunch raised a thin brow at me. "Just tell him, Mr. Timmons."

He strode up the stairs, leaving me alone with Lou. As I passed her on my way to the bike rack,

I thought she might have opened her mouth to say something.

I wasn't about to stick around long enough to find out what it was.

6

I had no idea what kind of deal Jack would have made with Mr. Bunch, but breaking it didn't sound like a good idea.

As I rode away from school, I thought I would go on down to our usual meeting spot, an abandoned dock on the river. Maybe Jack would be there, waiting for me. Then I remembered the high waters from last night's storm and realized that the dock would probably be underwater for a day yet.

I kept my eyes peeled for him as I rode onto Poplar Street. I waved as I passed Pastor Douglass leaving the barbershop, his face newly shaven. Mrs. Ballentine, the librarian, was just coming out of the library. I hurried past, because I knew if she saw me she would want to talk in that friendly way she had. But seeing her only reminded me of the Musgraves' empty farmhouse, so I had nothing kind to say in return.

At the filling station, Billy Updike was helping a man I didn't know with his map. The ice truck was parked outside Dinwiddie's General Store, and a mother walked out, toting groceries for supper in one arm and a wailing toddler in the other. But no Jack.

I was heading for the *Herald* office. Mama would be there, and I was hoping Jack would have already stopped in with an explanation for missing the paper route. I knew disappointing Mama wouldn't sit well with him.

Mrs. Hooper, the secretary, looked up as I stepped into the office. "Well, howdy, partner," she said, winking at me from behind her glasses. Mrs. Hooper had a small grandson named Tommy who loved cowboys, and she seemed to think I did, too.

The Christmas before, she had bought me a set of little tin cowboys. I was much too old for that kind of toy, but Mama said that Mrs. Hooper must have gone to a whole lot of trouble to find them, since all the tin being made was now being used in the war effort. She made me bring them the next time I came to the office. Ever since, Mrs. Hooper had asked me the same question.

"How's life in the Wild West, Danny?"

"Just fine, Mrs. Hooper," I said a touch guiltily, thinking of the cowboys sitting with the rest of my scrap-metal collection. A sacrifice I had been all too happy to make.

She grinned. "Here to see your mama?"

"Yes, ma'am."

I could already see her, sitting at the desk in the back corner where Daddy used to sit. Newspapers were piled in tall stacks around her, and she looked deep in concentration, tapping a pen against her lip, chestnut hair coming loose around her drawn face. People always said we looked alike. I had the same chestnut hair, the same long face and freckled green eyes that always seemed too serious.

"Not long until you're a big brother now," Mrs. Hooper went on. Another wink, like this was a secret we shared. "I keep telling her it'll be a boy. I'm sure of it. I suppose you'd like that?"

"I suppose so," I said. Truthfully, I tried not to think too much about the new baby one way or the other, but suddenly I could see it. Me with a little brother, teaching him things the way Jack had taught me, making them look easy.

I had never minded when Mrs. Musgrave brought little Jordan over while she and Mama sat and had tea. I liked helping him with words he didn't know in the newspaper and showing him my baseball card collection. Maybe I *would* like the baby to be a boy.

"Well, you can go on back," Mrs. Hooper said, waving her hand in invitation.

Most of the other desks in the office sat empty. Mr. Sawyer had enlisted right after Pearl Harbor, and Mr. Hataway had been drafted a few months back, just after Daddy had enlisted.

That was the way it was in Foggy Gap those days. Nearly all the men had gone to fight, or else moved off to where they could earn a better wage sewing parachutes or assembling tanks or cobbling combat boots, finding their way west or north, like the Musgraves had. But of course, the Musgraves had their own reasons for leaving, which had nothing much to do with wages, and everything to do with folks like Mrs. Ballentine and Mr. Pittman.

Besides Mama and Mrs. Hooper, the only other person working in the office that day was Mr. Ogletree, who had probably been too old to fight in the Revolutionary War. He had nodded off at his desk, arms crossed over his chest.

"Hi, Mama," I said, keeping my voice low so as not to disturb his nap.

She looked up, and her face broke into a wide smile. She brushed the hair back from her face and put down her pen. "Hi, Danny," she said. "How was school?"

"Fine," I said. No need to mention my lunchtime

detention or the scolding Mrs. Pattershaw had given me.

Though I knew Mama's accent—flat as the land she'd grown up on—had made her somewhat of an outsider in our little mountain town, her voice always calmed my nerves. I liked the way it was crisp and even, like the voices you heard on the radio.

"Jack never showed up this morning," I said. "I had to do his route, too. Have you seen him?"

Mama's brows furrowed into the shape of two little question marks.

"No," she replied. "That's strange. I don't think Jack's ever missed his route before."

"He hasn't."

"Maybe he's been taken ill," she suggested, tapping her pen against an article she'd been reading in some other newspaper. An issue of *New Republic* magazine was splayed open by her right elbow, next to *The Nation*. Daddy had read several national magazines every week ("to keep the pulse of things"), and now Mama read them, too.

"But he's never sick," I said. "I think . . . I think I need to go to his place. To see if he's okay."

Mama was shaking her head before I had even finished. "Mr. Bailey might be there. And I'd sooner you walked into a bear's den, Danny."

"But, Mama, it's *Jack*," I argued. "What if something's happened?"

Mama hesitated, then reached across the desk and

swept my own hair out of my eyes. Her fingers were ink-stained, and hardened from all the years of scrubbing and sweeping and cooking, but her touch was always gentle.

"You're right," she said. "But I can't let you go on your own. I'll come, too. Let me just get my things."

"All right," I said. Though I would never have admitted it, I was relieved that Mama was coming with me.

As she got up to gather her purse and coat, I glimpsed a word in the headline of the article she had been reading. WARSAW.

I knew Warsaw was a place in Europe, but I couldn't remember much else about it. If it was anything like its name, it would be hard and cold.

Not unlike the place we were going next.

7

Jack and his father lived in a cabin on the outskirts of town. It was set up on a little hill, which was a good thing because if it had been on low ground, it surely would have been swept away in the Great Flood three years ago. Even now, it looked like it was considering slipping right down off its perch and into the valley below. I had only ever seen the house from a distance— Jack never invited me any closer—but I knew from what he'd told me that it didn't have electricity or even running water.

Mama parked our car at the bottom of the hill and huffed as we climbed it. "Weren't you out with Jack last evening?"

I nodded. I had made it home just before dinner, as the storm had begun in earnest.

"Well, how much can have happened to him since then?" she asked.

I didn't answer. The question hung in the air like another storm waiting to break.

On one side of the cabin, the outhouse stood not quite far enough away, a little crescent moon carved into its door. On the other side was a rusty old flatbed truck with cinder blocks instead of tires. Attached to the truck's bed was a clothesline that had collapsed—underthings and all—into the mud. In front of the cabin was a water pump and a firepit full of ash.

"Hello?" Mama said. "Anyone home?"

My heart hopped around my chest like a frog on hot concrete.

"Jack?" I called. "Jack, are you in there?"

From inside the house came the sound of howling. That would be Winnie, the hound dog Jack had been given by Mr. Coombs as thanks for saving his daughters. I could hear her scratching at the door just before it burst open.

Mr. Bailey stood there, face twisted into a scowl, blinking against the afternoon light. He was wearing only blue jeans, which hung off his rail-thin frame. What little hair he had was tousled and gray. When his eyes landed on Mama, the scowl only deepened.

"I was asleep," he said.

It was only then that I noticed the long rifle resting next to the front door.

"I'm sorry to bother you, Mr. Bailey," said Mama crisply. "We came to see if Jack was all right. He missed his route this morning."

Winnie watched me from behind his legs, tail whirling around like a wind vane in a storm. Mr. Bailey paid her no mind. A rattling sound rose up from his throat, and then he spat into the bushes beside the cabin. His eyes narrowed.

"You come for nothing, then," he said. "I haven't seen that boy since yesterday morning."

"Are you certain?" Mama asked.

Mr. Bailey snorted as he emerged from the doorway. Winnie tried to worm her way around him, but he gave her a swift kick. A yelp, and then the door slammed as he stepped onto the porch. The whole house shook, and something in me shook with it.

"You people," he said, a growl shadowing his words, "think you're so much better than me. Think I can't even look after my own boy. Think I don't know what day it is."

"That's not it, Mr. Bailey," Mama replied. "That's not why—"

"You all think he's so *good*," he said, spitting the last word out like it had spoiled. "Too good for the likes of me, huh?"

Winnie had appeared in the window of the cabin,

scratching at the glass with her paws and whining.

My mouth had gone dry. Mama put a hand in front of me and started to back away, but Mr. Bailey kept walking toward us.

"If my son's so good, then where is he?" His eye twitched, his lip curled in a snarl.

"I don't know where he is," I mumbled.

"Then you're no good to me neither," said Mr. Bailey. "So get off my property and don't come back."

Mama pushed me toward the car and started up the engine as quickly as she could. I looked back as we drove away.

Mr. Bailey was still standing there, cracking the knuckles of one hand into the other, like he was fixing for a fight.

Before

October 1941

After Bruce and Logan had ridden off, it took me a moment to realize that Jack was reaching his hand out to shake mine. I met his grip and felt that my own hand was still trembling.

"I'm Danny," I said. "Danny Timmons."

"You sure you're okay? Breath coming back now?"

I tried to take a deep breath as an experiment. Air filled my chest. "Yeah," I said. "I'm fine now, thanks to you. You really aren't scared about Mr. Pittman?"

I was thinking of what Bruce had said—that his father would make Jack sorry.

But Jack shook his head. "He's had it in for me ever since I jumped in the water for those little girls," he said. "I reckon he didn't like being made to look like a coward. This won't change nothing."

I wanted to tell Jack then how much we had in common. I wanted to blurt out the whole story about the camping trip and the ghost stories and the trick the older scouts had played. I wished I could tell him that I wasn't the only one who had cried. Bruce had, too.

But the next morning, Bruce had pretended like it was just me who had been afraid. And I always had a feeling that it was precisely because I had seen Bruce cry that he had decided to tell everyone at school what a sissy I was. Because who would believe me then?

But I didn't say any of that. Jack gave me a gentle slap on the back, then began to walk away. I felt like I had missed my chance somehow.

"Hey!" I called. "Hey, wait!"

Jack turned, squinting into the sun. "Yeah?"

"Maybe—maybe you could teach me how to do that sometime," I blurted.

He kept staring at me. "You know, scare the daylights out of someone. Be . . . brave like that."

Jack took a step back toward me, and for a moment, that hard, fierce look flashed across his face again. For a split second, I felt afraid of him.

"Brave, huh?" he repeated. "You think scaring kids is the same as being brave?"

He said this like he wasn't just a kid himself, only

a couple years older than me. Then he shook his head.

"I helped you out because I hate bullies," he said. "But only a bully likes making someone afraid, Danny."

It was a cool day, but I felt shame baking my cheeks. I knew better than anyone in the world just how right Jack was.

"Sorry," I mumbled. "I just meant—thanks, I guess."

"Well, you're welcome," Jack said, his voice more gentle this time. "Maybe best we leave it at that, huh?"

As he walked away, he shook out his hand as if he had a writing cramp.

Only then did I realize something. It hadn't been my hand I'd felt trembling when I had shaken Jack's hand.

It was his.

8

June 1943

That night, though Mama had piled my plate high with pole beans from our victory garden, stewed apples, and pork chops, I could barely eat. On a normal night, I could have wolfed down a pork chop in a minute flat, especially now that meat had been rationed and we didn't eat it much anymore. But my guts felt all twisted up.

"Mama, I'm worried," I said, finally setting down my fork.

She sighed, and I saw that she hadn't touched her food, either. "I am, too, Danny. Any other boy his age, I'd be sure he was just playing hooky in the woods somewhere. But not Jack. He's too—too—"

"Good," I finished quietly.

"Yes."

Mama looked out the window to the quiet street, like maybe Jack would just come walking up our drive.

"Then why did Mr. Bailey say he wasn't?"

Mama's lips pursed. "You should know better than to listen to what Mr. Bailey says."

I did know better. And yet . . .

"He said he hadn't seen Jack since yesterday morning."

If that were true, it would mean I might have been the last one to see Jack before he'd gone missing.

"Yes," said Mama slowly, "but I wouldn't be surprised if Mr. Bailey were . . . confused . . . about that. Maybe Jack went too far up the mountain hunting this morning and got lost. I bet that's it."

"Jack?" I asked. "Get lost?"

There were places on the edge of town where forest gave way to wilderness, like rivers spilling out to sea. But Jack knew them better than anyone.

"Well, maybe he sprained his ankle and needs to rest it before getting back down," said Mama. "That same thing happened to Billy last fall, remember?"

"Maybe," I said. Though I also remembered Daddy saying that Billy just wanted a night's peace and quiet away from Mrs. Updike.

And there was a little voice in the back of my mind

telling me that Jack couldn't have gone hunting. That something about that story didn't add up. I just couldn't put my finger on what it was.

"If he doesn't show up for his route tomorrow, I'll have a word with the police," said Mama.

"And I'll come, too."

Mama gave me a searching look. "All right, then," she said. "*We'll* go to the police. But I'm sure it won't come to that. Now eat your dinner before it gets stone-cold."

And even though I wasn't hungry, I did. In war, *waste* was a word quickly lost.

9

That night, I sat on my bed for a long time and looked at the map I had pinned to my wall.

Shortly after we had entered the war, President Roosevelt asked every American family to buy a map of the world. We were lucky that there was already one at the *Herald* office, because by the next day there wasn't a map or globe to be bought in the entire state of North Carolina.

In his next fireside chat, President Roosevelt had come over the radio and talked the nation through where to find different places, explaining what was happening in each one. I hung our map on my wall the next day, and it had been there ever since.

Now I scanned the map until my eyes landed on *WARSAW*—the name I had seen in Mama's paper that afternoon. It was a city in Poland. Hitler's invasion of Poland was what had started the war in Europe in the first place, and as far as I knew, the Germans were still there. Which meant that whatever newsworthy thing had happened in Warsaw probably wasn't good.

I let my eyes drift further south and then west. Greece. Italy. France. "The battlegrounds of democracy," I'd heard someone say on the radio. Daddy would be there somewhere.

I kept the map up on my wall so I could feel closer to him. But that night I only felt farther away, looking at all those different countries and cities and rivers and mountain ranges I had never heard of. I thought of the gold star in the window of Dylan Price's house and shuddered.

If only I knew where Daddy was. If only I knew he would make it back safe.

I reached for the drawer of my bedside table and pulled out the book inside, *A Beginner's Guide to Morse Code*. Daddy had given it to me before he left. He had learned Morse code from his father, who had been a stationmaster. That was the reason Daddy had gotten to travel the railways for free when he was younger, which was how he'd met Mama.

Though I wasn't much good at basketball or

running, I *was* good at codes and puzzles. Daddy and I used to arrange my baseball card collection—by the player's height, or the last letter of the player's first name—and see if the other could guess how they were organized.

So every night I practiced Morse code before bed, pretending Daddy was looking over my shoulder. That evening, though, the little dots and dashes seemed to blur before my eyes. After a while, I set the book aside and turned off the light.

My mind wandered all the way from the battle-grounds of democracy back to Jack. I tried to imagine where he might be, but my mind remained stubbornly blank.

If only I knew where *Jack* was. If only I knew he would make it back safe.

Instead, an image of the Baileys' cabin came to me. Jack's home, if it could really be called one.

The Baileys were far from the only family in Foggy Gap living under a tin roof with no electricity or indoor plumbing. It wasn't those things that made me cringe. It was the collapsed clothesline and muddy under things. Winnie whining inside.

It was Mr. Bailey's face, a scarlet twist of rage.

It was the rifle by the door, like a giant rusty nail sticking up from the porch boards.

The rifle.

That was why Jack couldn't be out hunting. If he had gone hunting that morning, he would have taken the rifle with him.

Just like that, the thin hope that I'd been clinging to seemed to evaporate like a morning fog on the mountain ridge. Darker thoughts crowded in. Thoughts about Mr. Bailey, and about his hands. His rage.

About the rifle.

Before

December 1941

I didn't have much to do with Jack Bailey for a couple of months after he saved me from Bruce Pittman. Well, he *didn't have much to do with* me. If we crossed paths coming or going from school, I kept my head down and walked on by. I felt I had done something wrong that day with Bruce. Like I had glimpsed something in Jack I wasn't supposed to, and maybe revealed a part of me he hadn't wanted to see, either.

That all changed one Sunday evening in December, when Mama and I went to take Daddy supper at the Herald office, where he was working late.

By the time Jack knocked on the door, it was dark outside. I was slumped in Mrs. Hooper's chair reading, *while Mama copyedited an article for Daddy.*

When I first heard him knocking, the sound was so gentle I thought it might have been a bird. And when I looked up and saw him there, I didn't recognize him immediately. I didn't move from Mrs. Hooper's chair.

"Oh my Lord," Mama said behind me.

She seemed frozen for a moment, too. Then she rushed to the door. Daddy followed at her heels. Cold December air blew in with Jack.

Blood was gushing from his nose, and one of his eyes was swollen nearly shut. He seemed woozy on his feet.

I moved out of the way just in time for Daddy to help Jack into the chair I'd been sitting in.

"Are you all right, son?" Daddy asked, kneeling down so he could better assess Jack's injuries.

"Of course he's not. Look at the state of him. I'll go get some things to clean him up." Mama swept past us, toward the washroom.

"I'm sorry," Jack mumbled. His words were strange and heavy, like he was talking with his mouth full. "I came to see Dr. Penny but . . ."

He sniffled instead of finishing the sentence. It was Sunday, and Dr. Penny wouldn't have been in his office. The Hilltop Herald *would have been the only business on Poplar Street with light shining from its windows.*

"Just try to relax," Daddy counseled. "You're in good hands now."

Mama rushed back with a bowl of water and some

rags and began to clean the blood from Jack's face. She handed him a damp rag to put over his bad eye.

"Thank you," Jack said thickly. "I'll . . . I'll be all right now."

He tried to stand, then winced, bringing a hand to his side. He had no coat on.

"Sit down," Mama commanded. "And pull up your shirt."

When Jack hesitated, Mama gingerly lifted his shirt up on the side he'd been holding. I gasped. The skin was marbled with purple and blue, dark as the Appalachian twilight outside.

Mama sucked in her breath, too, and shared a look with Daddy.

"Jack," Mama said, her voice soft now, "did your father do this?"

Jack clutched the damp rag more tightly to his face. "He doesn't mean it," he whispered.

"Well, that's not going to make those injuries heal any faster."

"I shouldn't even have come," Jack whispered.

"Thank goodness you did," Mama said. "We can't let you go back there tonight. You'll come home with us."

"The car's outside," Daddy added. "Come on, we'll help you."

Jack opened his mouth to argue but let out a dry sob instead.

Ever since I'd caught sight of Jack standing out there

in the cold, I had been overcome by the oddest feeling, like someone was trying to shake me out of a dream. Finally, I realized that I should be helping, too. I moved to support Jack's left side, while Daddy kept him steady from the right. As I ducked under his shoulder, Jack glanced down at me with his good eye.

"Hiya, Danny," he managed to murmur as we made our way out into the night.

Mama made up the guest bedroom for Jack that night, just down the hall from me. I hardly slept a wink.

Though Daddy never laid a hand on me, I knew other kids had fathers who did. Lou's daddy had been known to make her go out and find her own switch from their hemlock grove.

But I had never seen anything like what Mr. Bailey had done to Jack. Never seen the vicious shade of purple that seeped like poison into his side.

I couldn't think of anything a boy could do that would be bad enough to earn him such punishment.

Finally, I got out of bed and tiptoed onto the landing. The air was a cold whisper against my cheek. I crept to the end of the hall and listened at Jack's door, but there was no sound from inside the room.

There were voices coming from somewhere, though. Light floated up from downstairs. I stole to the top of the staircase and listened.

"We'll call on Dr. Penny first thing in the morning," Mama was saying.

"Once we see what the damage is, I'll pay John Bailey a visit," Daddy replied, an unfamiliar hardness to his voice.

"You don't think we should go to the police?"

"They're not likely to get involved. Especially since Sergeant Womack is old friends with John."

"But the state of that boy, Alan. I don't need Dr. Penny to tell me what I can see with my own eyes. John Bailey could have killed him."

A chill wrapped itself around me, and I longed for my warm bed. I suddenly wished I had never left it.

10

June 1943
SATURDAY

The next morning, I woke up and got dressed before the sun rose. Mama hadn't risen yet, either, but she'd left out some bread and stewed apples from yesterday.

Mama had said we would go to the police that day if Jack didn't show up for his route again. As I ate, I thought about what I would say to them. Should I tell them the fears that had come to me in the night, about what Mr. Bailey might have done?

I took my time biking into town that morning, stopping to pick up a large nail someone had dropped. I'd add it to my scrap-metal collection when I got home. But the nail only reminded me of the rifle, so I tried to think of something else.

The air was dewy and silver, the sky above the mountains more like a still sea.

I had only seen the sea once a few years back, when Mama—who had spent summers on the ocean—was homesick for it. We rented a house tucked into the dunes and spent all day on the beach making castles and wading in the surf. Mama swam out much farther than me, to where she could float on her back beyond the breaking waves.

"Come on, Danny," she'd say, splashing golden droplets of water my way. "You'll love it out here."

With each passing day, I'd assured myself that the next day would be the one when I would be brave enough to accompany her. But every morning, I was still too afraid of being sucked out by the tide.

I'd cried silent tears half the way home, angry and ashamed that I had missed my chance to swim in the ocean. But for weeks afterward, I dreamed of kicking off the sand only to be swept from my feet by a force too deep and powerful to fight against.

That was how I felt as I biked into town. Like I was slowly swimming into a current that would pull me to a place I did not want to go. One that I might not be able to return from.

Nothing was open so early on a Saturday morning. The only person I passed was Billy Updike, who honked at me from his truck as he headed out of town to deliver his papers.

When I arrived at the *Herald*, there was no one in the parking lot. Mine and Jack's stacks of papers sat just outside the door.

I waited for a few long moments as the morning brightened and my hope dimmed. But Jack did not come.

And even though I had known deep down that he would not, I still felt his absence as a bitter loss. Standing there by myself, I had never felt quite so alone.

Before

December 1941

I hadn't realized how lonely I had been until Jack came to stay.

Of course I knew our house was quieter than, say, Lou's place, where there was always a baby screaming or someone arguing over the last slice of cake. I knew her house with its five children was more normal than mine. But I told myself that I liked the quiet better.

It was different when Jack was staying. There was a shift in the air, a current instead of stillness. The doors sprang open at a touch. The fire in the coal furnace crackled higher, and Daddy didn't have to go down to the basement to stoke it so often.

The house felt more alive with Jack there, even the

first few days when he couldn't do much besides lay in bed and listen to me read the funny pages while he slurped up the soup Mama brought him.

Dr. Penny had come that first morning, and I listened from the hall as he diagnosed Jack with a broken nose, two cracked ribs, and "a helluva black eye." This diagnosis had been delivered with a deep frown and a sideways glance at Daddy, who leaned in the doorway.

"Will Jack be staying with y'all for a while?" he asked.

"Yes," Daddy said. "As long as he likes."

Dr. Penny reminded me of a heron with his long legs, gray suit, and hunched back. All except his eyes, which were round and piercing as an owl's. He turned them to Jack. "You okay with that, son?"

Jack nodded.

Dr. Penny looked at Jack for another long moment. "Right," he said. "Well, that's that, then. Rest up now, you hear? I mean it." He packed up his things to go, then turned to Daddy. "Alan, can I have a word downstairs?"

When Daddy and Dr. Penny had finished talking in low voices, Daddy shrugged on his coat and went straight over to talk with Mr. Bailey. When he returned an hour or so later, he announced that Jack would be staying for a while.

"Are you sure?" Jack asked, sitting up too quickly

and grimacing. "You mean my father agreed?"

"He wasn't happy about it," Daddy said, sounding weary. "But in the end he agreed."

"Thank you, Mr. and Mrs. Timmons. I'll try not to be a bother, promise."

"You'll do no such thing," Mama said, fixing Jack with the look she gave me when she was not to be trifled with. "You're a guest in this house, which means you can bother us for whatever you need. Danny here will make sure you get it. He'll keep you company while you're laid up, won't you, Danny?"

And I had.

Jack and I sat in silence for an awkward moment after Mama and Daddy left us that first afternoon. My tongue felt knotted in my mouth. What could I possibly say that would be interesting to Jack Bailey?

He spoke before I could think of anything. "You got any cards?" he asked.

"Like baseball cards?"

He cracked a smile. It didn't do much to improve his battered face, but I didn't feel quite so nervous after that. "Well, I meant the playing kind, but baseball cards sound all right."

We spent the morning looking through my cards and marveling at the skills of guys like Joe DiMaggio, Dizzy Trout, and Ted Williams, who had batted .406 that season. We talked about how the Yankees could have blown the World Series so bad and whether they could win this year's.

And after that, things were easier between us. There was so much I wanted to ask Jack. What had it felt like to save the Coombs twins? To live without fear of drowning or bullies? And why had his father done this to him?

But I remembered how Jack had reacted the last time I had asked him a question, so instead we stuck to talking baseball, or playing gin rummy and arguing over the rules. When I went back to school on Monday, I brought his homework for him and worked on my own from the chair in his room. I watched from the corner of my eye as he ran his hand back and forth through his hair until he threw aside his pencil in frustration.

"Numbers don't make no sense, Danny," he said.

Numbers, like codes, had always made sense to me. And though he was in the ninth grade, and I was only in sixth, when I looked at his paper, I understood some of it and helped him where I could.

"You some kind of whiz kid?" he asked afterward, shooting me a grin. I noticed one of his bottom teeth was chipped.

"No," I mumbled. "Just good at math is all."

"That's nothing to be ashamed of," he said. "That why Bruce Pittman gives you trouble? Because you're good at school?"

I was glad to know that Jack, at least, hadn't heard

the story of the camping trip.

"He just always has," I said. And he probably always would. Though, now that I thought about it, in the two months since Jack had pinned him up against the dugout, Bruce hadn't tried to chase me down or embarrass me in front of the other kids at school.

And I realized I had Jack to thank for that.

When Jack had been with us a week, he was strong enough to come downstairs, which is where we were that Sunday afternoon. Daddy, Jack, and I were starting up a game of spades in the living room while Mama sat darning one of my sweaters and listening to the Sunday symphony on the radio. She listened every Sunday because she said it was nice to remember that something existed other than country music, which made her head hurt.

But just as I dealt out the first hand, the symphony was cut short by a special broadcast, all the way from Hawaii. A place called Pearl Harbor. Mama's hands went still as the broadcaster spoke of an attack. Ships were being bombed.

When the broadcast was over, she switched the radio off and there was a long moment of silence.

"Those poor boys," Mama whispered.

"At least now we know," Daddy murmured. "Now we can face it."

In a way, though, I think Daddy had already known

some of what was to come. He had taken to staying up late with the shortwave radio and searching it for broadcasts from Germany. Once, I'd come down for a glass of water and seen him leaned in close to the radio, his hands steepled in front of his mouth.

Sharp words had snarled from the radio. I could see the fear in Daddy's face, and I was glad I hadn't studied German like he had. I quietly retreated upstairs.

But there was no retreat this time. The words from the radio were in plain English, even if there was nothing plain about them.

"What does this mean?" I asked, looking from Mama to Daddy.

It was Jack, though, who answered me.

"It means war, Danny," he said solemnly. I'd never seen him so pale, not even the first night he had come to stay. "Right, Mr. Timmons?"

"I'm afraid so," Daddy said. He was already reaching for his coat. "I've got to go to the office. Don't wait up."

Before that Sunday, none of us had ever heard of Pearl Harbor, but afterward it was all anyone could talk about. By Tuesday, half the men in town had already enlisted. The streets and the radio and even the classrooms at school were full of talk of revenge and victory.

All that week, Daddy put in long hours at the Herald, and then he stayed up late into the night with Mama, talking in voices just quiet enough not to carry beyond the door, where I sat listening. When they began to argue in whispers, I returned to my room and pulled the covers over my head.

In my dreams, I saw flashes of red and felt the march of a thousand boots shaking the earth like thunder. I woke up shivering with sweat. One night, when I couldn't get back to sleep, I crept into the hall and saw a dim light shining from under Jack's door. I knocked softly.

"Come in."

He was sitting by the window, looking out at the moonlit trees, and there was a yearning in his eyes. Like he was a bird trapped in a cage.

"You couldn't sleep, either?"

I shook my head. He gestured toward the bed, so I crept across the room and sat down atop the quilt. Cold air slipped in through the cracks in the window, and I shivered.

"I think my daddy wants to enlist," I said. "But Mama doesn't want him to go." What else would they have stayed up so late arguing about?

Jack turned away from the window. "I bet you don't want him to go, either, huh?"

"I'm afraid, Jack," I said. "Why isn't anyone else afraid?"

He didn't say anything for a long minute.

"They *are* afraid," he said finally. "Every last one of

them. People just got different ways of showing fear, that's all."

"What about you? Will you fight if it goes on long enough?"

"Not if my father has anything to say about it," Jack said. "He'd want to keep me home as long as he can."

"I'd go," I blurted. "I'd fight if I was old enough."

I wasn't sure why I said it. Maybe because Jack was the only boy in town who didn't think I was a sissy, and I wanted to prove him right. Or maybe because I wanted to believe my own words. That, though I might be afraid now, I would have the courage when it counted.

Jack didn't seem impressed in the least by my declaration. "Well, I'm glad you aren't old enough, then." He turned back to the window. "Snow's coming soon."

Jack was right about the snow. It was hard to believe war was coming when the world looked so pure and clean. Jack and I made half a snowman in the backyard before Mama ran out in her house slippers, yelling that Jack needed to get back inside and back to resting those ribs.

"Yes, ma'am," Jack said, but I saw how it pained him to return to the house.

As if to bribe him into staying still, Mama brought us endless mugs of hot chocolate and bowls of steaming soup and set us to making paper chains and popcorn garlands for the Christmas tree that we would soon chop down. I was worried Jack might think this tradition too childish, but he took happily to cutting and gluing the paper rings, humming along to the carols on the radio.

Mrs. Musgrave stopped by on Saturday afternoon, as she did every week, with little Jordan in tow. In addition to our usual butter and cheese, they brought us the last of the season's apples and a wreath made from laurel leaves, which Mama exchanged for a box of homemade fudge.

I didn't know what Jack would think when the Musgraves arrived. Jordan must have been wondering the same thing, for he eyed Jack's bruised face warily, holding on to the hem of Mrs. Musgrave's dress. But Jack simply flashed a peppermint stick and smiled as Jordan's eyes widened. Before long, he was sitting between us on the sofa, sucking on his candy as Jack and I helped him make his own paper chain.

And the Musgraves weren't our only guests that day.

Not fifteen minutes after they had left, after Mama had insisted I take Jack up to rest, she suddenly ushered Lou into his room. Poor Lou had been stuffed into a red dress with white bows around the collar and the skirt, and she looked furious.

"Nice dress," I said.

"You shut your big mouth," she retorted. "Mama is making us go into Asheville to get family portraits before George joins up with the army."

Jack laughed, and she fixed her glare on him. He put his hands up innocently. "I didn't say a word."

"So, this is where you've been hiding," she said dramatically, turning her gaze to me. "I thought you mighta had the measles or something."

In those days, I usually biked over to Lou's first thing on a Saturday morning so we could go look for salamanders or play hide-and-seek beneath the hemlocks. The way friends do.

"I'll take the blame," Jack said.

Lou studied him. "What happened to you?" she asked. "You look like a vulture's dinner."

I wanted to tell Lou to shut her big mouth, but Jack just laughed again. "Bet I look worse. What've you got there?" He gestured to a wrapped present with a green twine bow Lou held underneath her arm.

"It's for you, Danny," Lou said, holding the gift out to me. "Your Christmas present. Mama said I had to give you one, but I say you have to give it back when you're done."

"Well?" Jack said when I didn't move. "Aren't you going to open it?"

I didn't need to open it to know what would be inside. The newest Nancy Drew book. I fidgeted in my chair.

Truthfully, I felt like I had outgrown Nancy Drew. I wanted to read about real grown-ups doing real spy work, not a girl playing detective. I hadn't had the heart to tell Lou, but no way did I want Jack Bailey to think I liked that stuff.

"I'll open it later," I said. "On Christmas."

"Aw, come on, Danny," Jack said. "It's the most excitement we've had in days. If you don't open it, I will."

I wondered, then, when the last time had been that anyone had given Jack a present. Slowly, I unwrapped the paper to reveal Nancy Drew and the Clue of the Tapping Heels.

"I haven't even read it yet," Lou said grandly, flopping down on Jack's bed and staring at the book with hungry eyes.

Jack studied it too. "What's it about?"

"Nancy Drew, of course," said Lou. "She's a detective. A sleuth. She's good at everything. Swimming and driving and riding horses."

I didn't mention that Nancy Drew was also well-dressed, usually well-mannered, and very popular. Lou often spoke about her as if she were a real person, a best friend. If Nancy Drew went to school with us, though, I thought Lou would probably be annoyed by her prim perfection. But then, people didn't really write books about girls like Lou. I supposed Nancy Drew was as close as she could get.

"And she always solves her cases," she was saying now. "When we grow up, Danny and I are going to start our own detect—"

"He just asked what it was about, Lou," I cut in.

"Sounds interesting," said Jack. "Why don't you read me some?"

"Really?" Lou and I said together.

"What else do we have to do? Anyway, I'd like to meet a girl who can swim and drive and ride horses and solve mysteries." He winked at me with his good eye.

Lou and I took turns reading until Mama called up and said that Mrs. Maguire was outside, and it was time for Lou to go take her portraits. She looked like she'd rather take an ice bath.

"Well, see you both later, I guess," she said. "You're all right, Jack Bailey."

"Don't forget to smile," I said.

She simpered, then pulled a face.

After she was gone, there was a moment of silence between me and Jack. Then: "Well," he said, "what are you waiting for? Keep reading."

Jack had been with us two weeks when Daddy decided it was time to get the Christmas tree. Even better, he convinced Mama that Jack was healed enough to go with us.

It had snowed off and on ever since Jack had arrived, and the ground was buried in several tiers of ice and snow, like layers of a cake. Daddy found an old pair of snowshoes to lend Jack, and the three of us trekked out into the forest, hunting for the perfect tree. Jack took the lead, barely leaving tracks in the snow as he went.

Most years, Daddy and I sang carols as we looked for the tree. We'd belt "Go Tell It on the Mountain," even though we could never remember the words after the first verse.

But this year, Jack kept up a steady stream of talk as we glided deeper into the forest. He shook the snow from the bough of a white pine and told us how you could both eat its bark and boil it down to put on a festering wound. We went past a sycamore tree with a hollow in its trunk so large Jack said a bear might very well be hibernating inside. A bit farther in, he pointed out the distant knot of a hawk's nest, high up in an enormous oak, and the turkey tracks beneath it.

"They love the acorns," he explained. "Nowhere better to look for a turkey than near a red oak."

He spoke of these things like I talked about my base-ball cards, and I understood that Jack's knowledge of the forest was its own collection, something he had worked hard to gather and was proud to share.

It took me awhile to realize that Jack was not just leading us but leading us somewhere. *Finally, we came* to a stop in front of a group of balsam trees clumped together like carolers, beside a craggy outcrop that offered a view of the white valley below.

"Here," he said, taking hold of one and shaking the snow off the branches. "What about this one?"

"Oh, I think that will do very nicely," Daddy said, nodding in approval. "Very nicely indeed."

Jack beamed at us, holding on to that tree like it was a blue ribbon at the county fair.

That afternoon Jack wasn't anyone's hero. He was just a kid at Christmastime.

We burst through the door with our treasure, laughing as we tried to shove the fat branches into the house. But the merriment died on our lips when we saw Mr. Bailey standing in the living room, shoulders hunched, face sour. Mama sat on the sofa, wringing her hands. She shot to her feet when we came in.

"Alan," she said, looking at Daddy. "Mr. Bailey just arrived. He—he wants Jack—"

"I'm taking my boy home," Mr. Bailey said. "Now." His eyes were trained on Daddy. He didn't so much as glance at Jack, and he hadn't even bothered taking off his cap. He was clearly not planning on staying around for a discussion.

"Wait just a minute here," Daddy said, hoisting the tree up against the wall and brushing stray needles from his hands. "Why don't you let Jack stay with us just a little longer? It's nearly Christmas."

"Christmas is a time for family," Mr. Bailey said flatly, "and that boy is mine."

Jack stood frozen in the doorway. His face—no longer swollen but still bruised—had gone blank. He stared at the coffee table, where our paper chains and garlands were coiled in neat piles, waiting for us to hang them on the tree. From the kitchen, I could smell ham baking.

"He's still healing," Mama argued, her voice sharp now. "He needs more time."

Mr. Bailey's lip curled, and he took a step toward Mama. "You don't think I know what my own son needs?"

He was too close to her. And though she drew up straight like fear was a foreign word, Daddy moved toward them.

"Now look—" he started.

But before he could say anything more, Jack had darted in front of his father. And there it was again—the hard look I had seen him give Bruce, the curl of his fingers into fists. For just a moment, he was every inch his father's son.

Then he let out a long, steady breath. "I'll go," he said. "My father's right. I should be getting home."

"But, Jack," said Mama, her face crumpling, "are you sure?"

"I'll be waiting outside," Mr. Bailey muttered.

He strode past us and out the door, slamming it shut behind him. Mama winced.

Daddy put a hand on Jack's shoulder. "If you don't want to go—"

"No, really," Jack said. "I should be going. He needs me. Besides, I miss Winnie. My dog. I've already left her alone too long. But thank you. For everything you've done."

He didn't have to go upstairs to collect his things because he had arrived with nothing. He had been wearing Daddy's old clothes while he stayed with us. But Mama wasn't going to let him leave empty-handed. She made him wait while she ran upstairs and returned with two shirt boxes.

"I didn't have time to wrap them," she said.

Inside the first box were two new flannel shirts. In the second was a pair of gray mittens, knitted by Mama. Something painful tugged at Jack's face as he ran his fingers over the mittens. His chin gave a wobble.

"Thank you, Mrs. Timmons," he said. "That was mighty kind of you."

"You'll start delivering papers in the new year like we discussed?" Daddy asked. He'd broached the subject on the way home from finding our tree. I had begged to have my own route, too, so Jack and I could start together.

"Yessir," said Jack. "I would appreciate that."

Only an hour ago, he had felt like a member of our family. A big brother who had come home for Christmas. Now he stood stiffly and spoke as though to a kindly stranger. The bright-eyed boy in the forest had gone, and the man in boy's shoes had returned. Even so, Mama wrapped her arms around his shoulders and squeezed him tightly.

"Take care of yourself, son," Daddy said.

I wanted to run to Jack and hug him, too. But I didn't move.

"Well, Merry Christmas," Jack said.

"Merry Christmas," I whispered.

And then he stepped out into the cold night, shutting the door behind him.

11

June 1943

"We shouldn't have let him go," I said quietly, as I thought back to that Christmas and of Jack disappearing out the door.

Now he had disappeared again.

Mama and I stood at the top of the stone steps that led up to the front entrance of town hall so she could catch her breath. The police station waited inside.

"Who?" she asked, resting a hand on her belly. In the other, she held a little package she had brought to mail to the Musgraves when we were done at the police station.

"Jack. We shouldn't have let him go back to Mr. Bailey."

Mama sighed, a stitch appearing between her

eyebrows. "It wasn't that simple, Danny," she said. "He's Mr. Bailey's son. And he *wanted* to go."

She sounded like she was trying to convince herself as much as me.

"Still," I mumbled.

"Still," Mama murmured.

Hearing footsteps climbing the stairs behind us, I turned to see a group of men. There was Dr. Penny with his narrow shoulders and blinking owl eyes, followed by a red-faced and huffing Mr. Maynard. Walking together behind him were Mr. Bunch and Mr. Pittman. Each of them wore a suit and tie and carried a briefcase under his arm.

Dr. Penny, who reached us first, tipped his hat at Mama. "Pearl," he said. "How are those ankles? Not too swollen?"

"They got me here," Mama replied, "so that's something."

The doctor frowned. "I want you to rest when you get home," he said. "I wouldn't want you to overdo so close to—"

"I'll do that, Doctor, thank you," said Mama.

Mama didn't take very kindly to being told what to do, not even by Dr. Penny, who she liked more than most folks.

"Hello, Pearl," said Mr. Maynard, heaving himself onto the landing. He shot a disapproving look at Mama's belly and didn't spare a glance for me.

"Hello, Mr. Maynard," Mama replied. "I did want another word with you about—"

"Sure, sure, but not right now," he said, waving a dismissive hand. "Draft board meeting, you know."

We did know. What else would those four men have been doing at town hall with their briefcases on a Saturday morning?

They were responsible for handling the draft in Foggy Gap. We all assumed they had been chosen because of their positions: Dr. Penny the doctor; Mr. Maynard the publisher; Mr. Bunch the school principal; and Mr. Pittman the biggest landowner. And because someone somewhere had decided they were the most important citizens in our town, these four men were now trusted to decide who was worthy of going to war and who wasn't, and who was needed even more at home.

Mr. Bunch and Mr. Pittman had reached the top of the stairs now.

"Good morning, Danny," Mr. Bunch said. "Did you manage to track down Jack?"

I remembered our conversation from the day before. The mysterious deal he claimed to have with Jack.

"No, sir," I said.

"What's this?" Mr. Pittman asked.

"I was just asking Danny here if he'd seen Jack Bailey," said Mr. Bunch. "He wasn't in school yesterday. No matter."

He tipped his hat at us and strode past.

"Huh. Is that right?" Mr. Pittman gave me a quizzical, almost amused, expression. I glared back. Mr. Pittman didn't look much like Bruce. He didn't have the dark hair or the freckles. Just the same small, mean eyes. I knew he wouldn't care about what had happened to Jack.

He gave Mama a smile as slippery and treacherous as a curve in an icy road as he held the door open. "After you, Mrs. Timmons," he drawled.

Mama's eyes narrowed.

Mama had her own reasons for disliking Mr. Pittman. She didn't like the way he was always trading his truck in for a newer, shinier one, and how he liked to drive slowly around town like he was in a parade. She complained about how he charged the sharecroppers who farmed his lands so much they had barely enough left to live on. But the thing that neither of us could forgive Mr. Pittman for was the way he had driven the Musgraves from Foggy Gap.

Now, though, she had no choice but to walk through the door he was currently holding open. "Thank you," she said stiffly, staring straight ahead.

"You remember what I said, Pearl," called Dr. Penny. "Get some rest when you get home."

The four men headed for a door on the opposite side of the hall. Watching them disappear, I felt a weight pressing on my shoulders.

I was just shy of thirteen. There was no file in any of those briefcases with my name on it. No one in that meeting would be discussing whether I should be given a draft card. Not for years to come, at which point the war would probably be over.

Although . . . when the war started, everyone said it would be over quick now that *we* were in it. But recently some folks had started to say it would go on until at least 1949.

Bruce talked about war like it was Christmas come early. Ever since the draft board was formed, he told anyone who would listen that his father was going to pull strings so he could enlist before he turned sixteen.

"I'd rather go to the army than the navy," he said, grinning. "At least in the army, they find your body if you die."

Mama said all that was hot air, but Bruce wasn't the only one who talked that way. Everyone acted like war was a party they couldn't wait to be invited to. The schoolyard was always home to battles fought with stick rifles and slingshots, and the lunchroom was full of talk about who would be the best spy, the best shot, the best soldier.

Ever since that night when Jack and I had spoken about the war, I kept trying to convince myself that what I had said was true. That I, too, would fight if my turn came. Once or twice, I had even slipped into the forest and pretended to be a soldier behind enemy lines, darting back and forth between the trees and peering out from ravines at my invisible foes.

But any mention of the war still made my throat clam up and my legs feel coltish. War made me dream in red and shook me awake at night. War sat leaden in my stomach, like a grenade that would one day detonate.

I felt a bit better when I remembered what Jack had told me. *They're all afraid.* And I *had* seen my neighbors going to church to pray at odd hours. I'd noticed the way folks held their breath and looked away whenever a dark car rolled into town, thinking of the black army car that showed up any time a boy or man had been killed or gone missing in action. Hoping if they looked away quick enough, it wouldn't stop outside their house.

And I had seen the way the other kids clutched their desks when Mr. Bunch had pulled Dylan from class, on the day that car had come for the Prices.

We had our own ways of showing it, like Jack said, but we *were* all afraid. Which meant that I was no different from anyone. I would have courage when it counted. In the meantime, I would collect scrap metal and go without sugar and tend our victory garden and do whatever else I could to help the war effort. That was something, wasn't it?

"Danny, are you coming or not?"

Mama stood outside the door to the police station, holding her little package.

"Coming," I mumbled. For a moment, I had nearly forgotten why we were there. Forgot that Jack needed me.

We stepped into a little waiting room where Officer Sawyer, whose father had worked at the paper before enlisting, sat behind a large wooden desk. He hadn't been an officer long. He was young and looked very tired, but the badges on his chest gleamed like they had been freshly polished. I wondered what had kept him from the draft. Club feet, maybe, or bad lungs?

He looked up as the door closed behind us.

"Morning, Pearl," he said to Mama. "How can I help you?"

"We're here to report a missing person," I said. Like a line out of Nancy Drew.

Officer Sawyer raised an eyebrow. I saw Mama's surprised glance from the corner of my eye.

"A missing person?" he repeated.

"Jack Bailey," Mama explained. "John Bailey's son. Jack delivers papers for us. But he hasn't shown up the past two days. I'm sure there's an explanation, but it's very unlike him."

"You need to go see Mr. Bailey," I said. I could feel

Mama's surprise give way to unease. But I had to speak aloud the terrible thought that had been tumbling around in my head.

"And why is that?" said Officer Sawyer, leaning forward and frowning.

"Because he's awful," I said, more loudly than I'd meant to. "Everyone knows he—"

"What's all this?"

Sergeant Womack had appeared in the doorway next to the desk. He was tall, with a narrow mustache and pox scars across his cheeks.

"Sarge," said the first officer. "Mrs. Timmons and Danny here are worried about Jack Bailey. Say he hasn't shown up for his paper route in two days."

"Hello, Mrs. Timmons," said the sergeant.

"Hello, Sergeant Womack," Mama replied evenly. "I apologize for the fuss, but Danny's very worried. We both are."

"Well, sure you are," said the sergeant. "You did the right thing coming to us. We'll get to the bottom of it, so don't you worry yourself anymore. Particularly not in your condition."

He looked away from Mama, like he was a bit embarrassed even to be seeing her in her "condition."

"So you'll interview Mr. Bailey?" I asked. "Search his house?"

The sergeant shared a little smile that Officer

Sawyer returned a bit reluctantly. "Interviews and searches? You're talking like you think a crime's been committed. Jack is probably somewhere in the woods just playing hooky. Or maybe he ran off to try to enlist early. Wouldn't be the first boy who jumped the gun."

"Jack wouldn't do those things," I said. A muscle in the Sergeant's face twitched.

Not without telling me, I added silently.

Though it wasn't as if Jack didn't have secrets. He had never mentioned his deal with Mr. Bunch, for instance.

I pushed that thought aside as a flicker of irritation crossed Sergeant Womack's face. "Well, like I said, we'll get to the bottom of it."

"Mr. Bailey's hurt Jack before," I said quietly, meaning to finish what I'd started. "And he's got a gun."

I heard Mama's sharp intake of breath. "Danny," she cautioned.

Sergeant Womack gave me a long look. He wasn't smiling any longer. "Lots of people have guns."

I remembered then what Daddy had said about Sergeant Womack being an old friend of Mr. Bailey's.

"Yes, but—"

He lifted a hand to stop me. It might as well have been a brick wall. "It's like I said, son. You leave this with us now. We'll take it from here."

Heat spread over my cheeks. I was not his son. And *my* father would want me to stand up for Jack. "Yes," I said, louder this time, "but—"

"Danny," Mama said again, her voice cracking suddenly through the air like the sound of a tree branch snapping. "That's enough. We've taken too much of these officers' time."

"Not at all," said Sergeant Womack. But his words were curt. "You have a good day, Mrs. Timmons."

12

Outside, *Mama folded herself* onto a bench in the little park next to town hall. She closed her eyes and rubbed her brow with her thumb and forefinger as if she were trying to smooth the wrinkles from her thoughts. I slumped down beside her. On the grass, two children were trying to hoist a homemade kite into the air.

"What got into you in there?" she asked, turning to me. Her eyes were searching, not angry.

My head was still buzzing with the rush of speaking up to Sergeant Womack. "Everything I said was true. And I'm not sorry I said it."

Mama sighed. "You as good as accused Mr. Bailey of being a murderer, Danny. That's a very serious thing to suggest."

"You should be on my side!" I retorted. "Jack's side, Mama."

She was still staring at me, eyes sharp and green as sea glass. "Do you really think Mr. Bailey could do something like that?"

I met her gaze. "Do you?"

One of the children in the grass began to shriek, making Mama jump. We both watched as the kite caught a momentary breeze, then crashed into the branches of a maple tree. Mama didn't say anything for a long moment. She seemed to be thinking. Maybe weighing how much truth I could hold on my shoulders.

"No," she said at last. "John Bailey is a hard man. There's no denying that. But I looked him in his eyes yesterday. There was anger there, but no sorrow. No regret. To take his own child's life and show no remorse? Killing *anyone* is a terrible enough thing. I just don't think he's capable of that. I really don't."

She swept one hand over her stomach and took mine with the other. She squeezed.

I knew she meant those words to comfort me. But all they did was make me realize that John Bailey was perfectly capable of taking another life.

Because, I remembered, he already had.

Before

January 1942

After Jack Bailey followed his father out into that cold December night, I didn't see him again for a while. I looked for him in church on Christmas Eve, but I might as well have been searching for Santa Claus.

And yet, he was with us as we decorated the tree and opened gifts on Christmas morning. He was the shadow cast over our songs and small talk. The icy breeze that blew down the chimney, shrinking our fire to embers. Every once in a while silence would fall between us and I knew Mama and Daddy were thinking of him just like I was, wondering if he was all right and what it would be like to spend Christmas with John Bailey.

Even Lou asked about him on New Year's Eve, when

the Maguires came over to drink a toast with us. We toasted to 1942. To winning the war. To Lou's brother, George, who had by then enlisted in the army and would soon be shipping out overseas.

It wasn't until we returned to school that I saw Jack again. The afternoon bell had rung, and I was fumbling with my gloved hands to untangle my bike from the others on the rack. Lou was doing detention for sticking her tongue out at our teacher after she'd been scolded for talking.

When I finally got the bike free, I turned to find myself face-to-face with him.

"Jack!" I said. "You're here! You're all right?"

"I'm fine," he replied. "You wanna go somewhere?"

He looked down at his worn shoes, shuffling them over the muddy ground. I realized that he was embarrassed.

"Yeah," I agreed, a little too eagerly. "I mean, sure. That'd be good."

Jack nodded. "Come on," he said. "I know a place."

I followed Jack and his rusty bike as we skirted around Poplar Street and then along to the river, to the place where the town locked arms with the hills and the paved road petered out into a dirt track. The wind whistled in my ears, turning them red with cold. When I breathed out, my breath was silver.

We left the track for an overgrown trail through the

forest. The snow had mostly melted from the ground by then, but little icicles still hung from the bare trees, making them flash in the low winter sun.

Finally, we came to a tangled den of rhododendrons that stretched as far as the eye could see. Their branches looked impenetrable to me, but Jack led us down a narrow tunnel through the deep green sea. The rhododendrons crackled and whispered around us in the murky darkness, but soon enough I could see the river was just ahead. It was frozen solid, shining like a giant ivory ribbon left over from Christmas morning. Jack pointed to a rickety dock.

"Told you I'd show you my fishing spot," he said. "It's a good swimming hole, too. No one ever comes here. I reckon the property was abandoned in the flood. But somehow this dock survived."

"Are we ice fishing?" I asked, propping my bike up on its kickstand, away from Jack's bike. I had gotten it for Christmas, and the blue paint gleamed a little too proudly next to the rusted metal of Jack's bike.

"I don't just come here to fish," said Jack. "I come here to think sometimes, too. When I need to get away."

He picked up a round river stone before walking to the end of the dock. He sat down and began turning the stone over and over in his hand. He was wearing the mittens Mama had made for him.

I took a seat next to him, cupping my own gloved

hands and blowing warm air into them. Jack's words felt like an invitation to ask the questions I had been wondering about for weeks now.

"It must be hard," I ventured. "Living with your dad?"

He threw the rock up into the air. "It's not easy," he said. "But it's not always . . . that bad."

"It looked pretty bad that night you came to stay."

Jack kept his eyes on the rock. "Yeah," he said. "But he's not a monster, you know. He taught me to hunt and fish. He can be all right sometimes. And I don't think he really means to—to hurt me."

At this, I raised my eyebrows. "Doesn't mean to?" How could someone accidentally do what John Bailey had done to his son?

Jack curled his hand around the rock again and stared out at the frozen river. "He don't know what he's doing sometimes," he said. "Not until after he's already done it."

"Oh."

I was stuck on the word sometimes. That meant this hadn't been the first time John Bailey had beaten his son. It meant that it might not have been the last, either.

"My mother used to say that he was a different person before the war," Jack said quietly. "That he was the most gentle man she'd ever met."

Jack meant the First World War. My own father had been too young to fight in it, but his older brother had gone and died in the trenches in France. Daddy didn't like to talk about it, but he kept my uncle's medal in a glass case in his office, always polished to a shine.

"So what happened?" I asked.

"War," Jack said. "The war happened. It got under his skin, like some kind of spell. He came back, and he was so different. My mother tried everything to help him, but nothing ever worked. She was gonna leave him, but then she found out she was going to have a baby. Me."

His eyes were glazed and shining, but there was a hardness to them too, just like the frozen river before us.

"So she stayed?"

"He'd always wanted to have a kid, but they never could. She thought he would have to change then. That I was going to bring him back, you know? But it didn't work. Like I said, nothing ever worked."

He threw the rock out onto the river, where it landed with a harsh crack! I winced. The ice held fast.

"Anyway, there's these times when he just . . . goes away. He starts yelling and hollering and swinging at anything that moves. That's what happened the night I showed up at your daddy's office."

"I'm sorry," I said meekly. I felt strange, like I had staring at Jack's bloody face. I shut my eyes. Everything felt too sharp, too bright, too bare. I didn't want to see it anymore.

"He was, too," said Jack. "My father. He's always sorry

when something like this happens. I guess it's just too hard sometimes, living with everything he saw. Everything he did."

"Everything he did?"

Jack looked at me for a long moment. "It was war, Danny," he said. "Kill or be killed."

13

June 1943

I wanted to go straight to the dock from the park. After the first day Jack took me there, we went back often. It became our usual meeting place, and it was also the last place I had seen him.

I was trying my best to believe Mama was right. That killing another man in war didn't mean Mr. Bailey could do the same to his own son. I told myself that I would find something at the dock, some clue that would tell me where Jack had gone.

But Mama needed to go to the general store—which doubled as the post office—to mail her package to the Musgraves. Though fuel was rationed, Mama had taken to driving into town as she'd grown larger. I decided it would be faster to wait for her to drive me home to get my bike than to walk there myself.

The bell rang as we entered the store, and Mrs. Dinwiddie looked up from behind the counter. She had been running Dinwiddie's General Store for as long as I could remember. And for as long as I could remember, she had looked old, yet she never really seemed to get any *older.* She was a round woman, with white bobbed hair and glasses that hung from a beaded chain around her wobbly neck.

"Mrs. Timmons," she said, smiling big at Mama. "What can I get you?"

The general store shelves weren't half as full as they used to be, and it always seemed like someone had just come in and gotten the last can of coffee, or bag of sugar.

But Mrs. Dinwiddie waved around at her goods— the stacks of cans here, the seed stand there, a display of combs atop the counter—like a queen gesturing to her riches. "Let me guess. Seltzer for your stomach? Epsom salt for your feet? No, that's not it, is it? You've got a craving for something, don't you? I wanted watermelon when I was expecting my youngest. Too bad he was born in February."

"Hello, Mrs. Dinwiddie," returned Mama.

"Go on, Danny," said Mrs. Dinwiddie, opening up the jar of licorice twists on the counter. She always let me have one for free when we came in. But I wasn't in a licorice sort of mood.

"No thank you," I said.

"Suit yourself. Come to think of it, I have something else for you two."

She turned behind her to the slots where the mail was kept and plucked a letter out, handing it to Mama.

"Oh! It's from your grandmother," she said to me as she opened it up and scanned it. "Confirming her train."

Granny Mabel was coming at the end of the next week to help Mama look after the baby. It would be the first time either of us had seen her in nearly a year, since Granny had taken a job in a munitions factory and never took a day off. She said it was her duty.

"You look tired," Mrs. Dinwiddie said, tutting at Mama. "You really shouldn't be working at a time like this."

Mama *did* look a little worn around the edges, whether from fatigue or worry, I didn't know.

"I'll keep that in mind," Mama said. "And actually, I've got a package here to mail."

She held up the little box, wrapped in brown paper.

Mrs. Dinwiddie crossed her arms and gave a little *harrumph*. "It's Saturday. The post office isn't open on Saturday. You know that."

"Of course," Mama agreed, her voice suddenly

buttery soft. "I wasn't thinking when we left the house this morning. You're right—I haven't been sleeping well. I don't suppose you could . . ."

Mama dropped her gaze down to her belly, and Mrs. Dinwiddie gave a sigh.

"Well, there's no harm in me taking it just this once. But it won't get mailed until Monday. Hand it over."

Mama straightened. "I do appreciate it," she said, passing the package across the counter.

Mrs. Dinwiddie glanced down at it. "The Musgraves?" she asked, reading the address. "You're still in touch with Daphne?"

"I'm still in touch with *Mrs. Musgrave*, yes," Mama said. "I thought I would send some strawberry preserves. A little taste of home."

"Well, that's kind of you," Mrs. Dinwiddie said, though it didn't sound much like she meant it. "It was such a shame, them deciding to leave. So many folks leaving these days."

"Well," Mama replied, her voice curdling, "they didn't exactly *decide* to leave, now did they?"

Mrs. Dinwiddie's nostrils flared, and she gave Mama an annoyed smirk. "Well, you tell them I say hello next time you write."

Mama huffed as we stepped back onto the street. "That family helped feed half this town from their farm during the Depression," she grumbled. "And look at how they were repaid. Boy, people sure do have short memories."

"Did you tell Jordan *I* said hello?" I asked Mama.

But she didn't seem to hear. Instead, she rounded on me. "Don't you forget, Danny," she said, "that you may have been raised in a small town, but you were *not* raised to have a small mind."

And I knew what she meant, because we had talked about small minds once before.

Before

1940–1942

It had been the Pittmans who had forced the Musgraves from Foggy Gap and from our lives. But it was also the Pittmans who had brought us together in the first place.

I'm not sure Mama and Mrs. Musgrave ever would have struck up such a friendship if it weren't for one autumn afternoon in 1940 when Bruce and Logan had chased me all over town, threatening to throw me in the Watauga, which was icy cold so late in the year. We hadn't yet entered the war, and I hadn't yet met Jack Bailey. So frightening me was still Bruce and Logan's favorite form of entertainment.

I had cut through one of the bits of forest that shot through Foggy Gap like veins in a piece of quartz, hoping to shake them. When I found myself on the other side of the wood, I looked over my shoulder to see if they were still following me. To my relief, it seemed they had given up. But it was because I was looking backward that I didn't see the rock in the road.

My tires skidded and I fell sideways, landing with a hard thud. A dagger of pain twisted through my ankle, and I accidentally bit my lip so hard I could taste blood. I heard distant laughter in the woods behind me.

When I got up, I couldn't put weight on my hurt ankle. I was standing there on one leg, trying to figure out how I was ever going to get home, when I heard a voice nearby.

"Are you all right?"

I turned to see Mrs. Musgrave standing at the end of her drive, a basket full of apples balanced in the crook of her elbow. Her brown eyes peered out from beneath the brim of her straw hat, under which she had tucked her shiny dark hair. Her cheeks were round and speckled and made her look like she was always about to smile, even when she was sorrowful.

Her voice was gentle. It was that tender voice that made a little sob burst from my lips.

Mrs. Musgrave shook her head. "Hush now," she said, her gaze flicking to the woods. "Don't you give him your tears. That's letting him win."

She must have heard Bruce's laughter, the meanness in it. I didn't know if she guessed who "he" was, but somehow I suspected she did. I lifted my chin and blinked away the tears.

She nodded her approval. "Now, what's happened to that leg?"

"I think I twisted my ankle."

"Can you walk on it?" she asked.

I stepped on it again and winced in pain.

"My Anthony is out with the truck," she said. "But I'll get the cart and take you home."

"I'll be fine," I protested, but she had already turned and was walking swiftly up the drive, taking care not to let the hem of her skirt brush against the ground.

As the Musgraves' cart rattled through town with their mare, Rosie, clomping ahead of it, a few folks waved or called hello. They greeted Mrs. Musgrave by her first name, Daphne.

When their eyes landed on me next to her, they cocked their heads, trying to make sense of me riding in the cart with her, my bike bouncing along in the back. She kept her eyes straight ahead, except to return a greeting with a friendly nod. Her back was straight as an arrow, her knuckles clenched tightly around the reins.

Mama was out front beating a rug when we arrived at the house. She did a double take when she saw the cart, then let the rug fall to the ground and came to meet us at the road. As I hobbled down, Mrs. Musgrave explained what had happened. Mama shot me a troubled look.

"Well, you'd better come in so we can see to that ankle," Mama said, lifting my bike from the back of the cart. "And you, too, Mrs. Musgrave. Come in and warm up. You must both be freezing."

"Oh—well—that's all right, Mrs. Timmons," Mrs. Musgrave replied, sounding surprised.

"Please," said Mama. "You've brought my son home safely. The least I can do is get you some hot tea."

Mrs. Musgrave glanced in either direction, then nodded. "Well, just for a few minutes, then." She got down from the cart, tying Rosie's reins to our fence post and patting her dappled neck.

Once we were inside, I said my thank-yous to Mrs. Musgrave and was guided upstairs, where Mama propped my leg up with pillows and wrapped icy wet towels around my ankle. She left the door open, and after a few minutes the sound of her conversation with Mrs. Musgrave drifted up to me. At first, the words were stiff and halting, but soon, I heard the chiming of laughter.

The voices flowed more smoothly then, and Mrs. Musgrave stayed far longer than the few minutes she had planned.

» «

After that, Mrs. Musgrave came by our house practically every Saturday afternoon, always with a basket or an old milk carton piled high with the dairy and produce Mama had ordered for the week.

If you asked her, Mama would say we got our goods from the Musgraves because their farm had the sweetest corn, the juiciest tomatoes, and the richest butter. But that didn't explain why Mrs. Musgrave, often accompanied by Jordan, always stayed for an hour or two, to talk to Mama over tea.

Even before Daddy left for the war, Mama sure needed the company. She might be welcome to Bible study, or to laugh with the other women at the Fourth of July picnic. But no matter how long she lived in Foggy Gap, she would never be one of them.

Most people still raised their brows at the way Mama spoke with her clipped, flat words, and sometimes they narrowed their eyes at the things she said. They were suspicious of the books she read, her dislike of country music, and of the fact that she was almost the only one of them who drove a car. Mama was just too different.

Mrs. Musgrave was different, too. Because if Mama's skin was pale as daisy petals, then Mrs. Musgrave's was dark as the center of a sunflower. And the Musgrave family was like a lone patch of sunflowers growing on a hillside full of daisies, for there were no other Black families in Foggy Gap.

Mama and Mrs. Musgrave were both outsiders in different ways, both lonely, too, and maybe that's why they became friends. And maybe that kinship was what made the corn taste so sweet, the butter so rich.

On those Saturday afternoons, I often ended up keeping little Jordan company. But he didn't like straying too far from his mama, so we would sit together in the hall just outside the parlor, where we could hear most of what our mothers said.

That was how I found out that Mrs. Musgrave had moved to Foggy Gap from another mountain town, Boone, where she had lived in a neighborhood she called "the Hill" with many other Black families. She had been a school teacher before she met Mr. Musgrave, who had only come to Boone to visit relatives but had left with Mrs. Musgrave on his arm.

I learned that Mr. Musgrave's family had owned his farm since just after the Civil War and that it was on hard, rocky land—land that had little patience for nursing roots and seeds. But over many years, the family had slowly coaxed the soil into growing a few things, and then a few more, until finally it was bursting with apple blossoms and squash vines, cornstalks and hay bales.

I overheard Mrs. Musgrave confide in Mama that she loved the farm and didn't mind the short nights and early mornings. But she missed her old life—singing in the church choir and eating Sunday dinners with family, before another week of teaching children who were as good as her own. Now, Jordan was her only student.

She was sure doing a good job of teaching him. Even though he wasn't school-aged yet, he could already read many of the words in the newspaper. He would always ask for a copy when they arrived, and I would sit with him in the hallway and help him when he couldn't sound out one of the words. Whenever he managed a particularly difficult one, like infamy or resistance, a light switched on in his eyes, and a grin took over his face that was hard not to share. He had the same round cheeks as his mother, only his were punctuated by a dimple on each side.

He didn't know the meaning of lots of the words. There were some I didn't know, either, though I did my best to pretend otherwise. Even though Daddy edited the paper, I thought the news was pretty dull. Up until we entered the war, at least. And I thought it was strange that a little kid like Jordan liked to read it so much.

One Saturday after the Musgraves had left, I said as much to Mama. She crossed her arms over her chest and gave me a long, searching look.

"Danny," she said, "you know what segregation is, don't you?"

I had heard Mama and Daddy discuss segregation before. Every time we went into Asheville and saw the signs all over town identifying the "white" and "colored" entrances, bathrooms, and water fountains, Mama would talk about the unfairness of treating people differently based on their color, like you could tell what was underneath from what was on the outside. You might as well try to judge the character of a nation by the color of its flag, she had said once.

But I also knew that most white folks didn't agree with her, which was why Asheville was full of those signs.

The Musgraves didn't live in a big city like Asheville, though. They lived in Foggy Gap, where there were no signs and everyone knew them. Hadn't folks called out to greet Mrs. Musgrave when we had ridden through town in her cart? Hadn't I seen Mr. Musgrave's tall, narrow frame coming and going from Dinwiddie's General Store many times over the years?

But then, I thought, there was the way that people referred to them as Anthony and Daphne, rather than Mr. and Mrs. Musgrave. And I had never seen them in the diner, or the barbershop, or at the swimming hole. I stared at Mama, understanding starting to sink into my skin like rain into the earth.

"But what's segregation got to do with Jordan reading the paper?" I asked.

"He reads the paper because he can't check books out from the library," Mama said. "Mrs. Ballentine won't allow the Musgraves in."

By then, my insides had been churned to sticky red clay. "Mrs. Ballentine—"

Mrs. Ballentine had brought a tall stack of books straight to our door two years ago when I'd had the flu, along with a homemade apple pie. She wrote every kid in town a birthday card every year. At least, I thought she wrote to every kid.

The deep furrow in Mama's brow softened, like she knew what I was thinking. "We can never see into another person's soul, Danny," she said. "And you just remember—nothing limits a big heart like a small mind."

14

June 1943

By the time Mama and I arrived home after mailing the package to Mrs. Musgrave, Mama's anger had faded to weariness, and she said that she needed to go upstairs and lie down. I told her I was going to go look for any sign of Jack.

"Well, I suppose that's all right," she said, "as long as you don't set foot anywhere near Jack Bailey's house again."

I jumped on my bike and raced off, abandoning the road at the first chance and choosing the narrow path that led under the pines and along the river. It was a warm day, and here and there people had laid out picnic blankets or set up fishing lines on the rocks that jutted out over the water.

Everyone I passed looked happy, like the sun had melted their cares away. I waved to Pastor Douglass, who was sharing a pint of strawberries with his children. I recognized many of the other people, too, from my route, or from school or church. Mama might have felt like an outsider in Foggy Gap, but I never had. Not even when Bruce set his sights on me.

I had been born in Foggy Gap. I had known it all my life. But ever since Mama told me about Mrs. Ballentine not wanting the Musgraves in the library, I started wondering just how well I understood my town. If someone as nice as Mrs. Ballentine could be so cruel, who knew what other ugliness hid in people's souls?

Could Jack have been hiding something, too? Not a prejudice, like Mrs. Ballentine held, but a secret? Something that might explain his disappearance?

I willed myself on faster. The farther I biked, the fewer people I passed. Finally, the path petered out behind me, and I could only hear the gentle current of the river and flurries of birdsong from the trees. When the ground became too rocky to bike on, I got off and trotted as quickly as I could through the rhododendrons that surrounded the spot like emerald shields.

My heart quickened at the sight of the crooked dock peeking through the leaves, like maybe I would simply find Jack waiting there, exactly where I'd left him two nights before.

But the dock was empty. The planks were soft and

slick underfoot. It seemed like the patches of moss that half covered them had grown thicker in the two days since I'd been there.

I looked around. The water, though still high, was calm and cheerful, and our secret swimming hole looked inviting. Across the river, fool's gold glittered along the wide, pebbly banks.

To the side of the dock was an enormous boulder that had a narrow crevice in it. I ducked down and peeked in through the crevice. Two wooden fishing rods and a tackle box were nestled inside, just like they usually were. Jack must have tucked them away after I'd left him that evening.

As I stood up, I glimpsed something on the far side of the boulder. The dull shine of old metal. At first, my heart leaped in the way it did when I spotted a tin can or something else for my scrap-metal collection. Then, as it sank in what I was seeing, cold prickles went up my spine.

Propped against a spruce tree was Jack's bike.

Which meant Jack must have left here on foot. But that made no sense. Why would he want to walk home in the rain?

There was another possibility. That he had never left at all.

My eyes darted instinctively to the river. I thought of the storm that had set in just as I had left Jack. The rain that had swelled the river past its banks, churning its plodding pace into the kind of current that could sweep you away so far so quick that you'd be a stranger where you washed up.

My fingers began to tingle. I felt suddenly hollow. Light enough that a breeze could sweep me far away, too.

Could the answer be as terrible—as simple—as that? I had worried Mr. Bailey was to blame for Jack's disappearance, but could the river have been the culprit all along?

I felt the cold of it, like I was the one being plunged in. Could I have ridden off and left my best friend to drown?

No, I reminded myself. This was *Jack Bailey*. Half the town had seen him dive in the floodwater to save the Coombs twins. I had seen Jack swim a thousand times, and there was nobody stronger in the water.

And yet . . . there was his bike. Why would he have left without it?

The bike was leaned up against the tree, exactly as I remembered it being that last evening. I checked the saddlebags, which were empty except for a couple of stubby pencils and a comb.

Then my eyes fell on the tree, and my heart lurched again.

Someone had carved a word into the bark.

Before

June 1942

"Where did your mother go?" I asked Jack one afternoon. "I mean, what happened to her?"

Spring was slowly thickening to summer, like cream being churned to butter. The rhododendrons behind us were all in bloom, the blossoms thick with bees.

Jack and I were lying on the dock, letting the sun warm our bare chests after plunging into the cold water. Now that the weather was nice, we came nearly every afternoon to swim or fish, or just to doze in the sun.

"She died," he said, sitting up on his elbows. "Pneumonia. When I was eight."

"Oh," I mumbled. It was silly, but the thought of her dying hadn't even occurred to me. I didn't know what to say. "I'm sorry. I thought maybe, you know, with your dad and everything—"

"You thought she left?"

I didn't answer. I wondered what was worse—to have a mother who left you or to have no mother at all. I thought of how Mama stopped me on the way out the door every morning to plant a kiss on my head. She had done it ever since first grade, when I started walking alone to school and was afraid of taking the shortcut through the forest.

"An old trick I learned," she'd said, a smile playing at her lips. "A mother's kiss is strong enough to ward off anything that wants to do you harm."

Even when she wasn't there, Mama found a way to protect me. She would never have left me alone with a man like Mr. Bailey.

"She never tried to take you away before she died?" I asked Jack. "She didn't have anywhere else to go?"

Jack, his face still tilted up toward the sun, let his eyes close. "No," he said. "We just . . . stayed. Except—"

The word hung uncertainly between us. The air hummed.

"Yeah?"

"Nothing," Jack said, opening his eyes and sitting upright. "It's stupid."

"You can tell me," I urged. "You can tell me anything."

"Well, there was a town she used to tell me about,"

he said finally, "on nights when things with my dad weren't . . . so good. She'd bundle me up and we'd go outside and lie down under the stars. She always promised she would take me one day."

"Where is it?"

He shrugged. "She told me it was downriver somewhere. Tucked way back in the forest. She said you could never stumble across it. You could only find it if you were looking for it."

"What kind of town?"

Jack stared at the river, the gray current filling his eyes. "A perfect town. The kind where there's never any trouble. Where they've never even heard of war. There's one long table that runs down the main street, so long you can't see from one end to the other. Everyone eats there together. On cold nights, they build fires and the whole town sits around and sings songs and tells stories. And when it's warm, they all sleep in hammocks tied to the trees."

I stared at Jack, waiting for him to burst into laughter, to tell me he was just kidding. But as he talked, his eyes grew wide and glittering and his words came faster and faster, like a train picking up steam.

"No one ever fights, see, because they have everything they need," he went on. "They got a stream with the sweetest water you've ever tasted. Fields of the richest soil. They can grow cornstalks tall as dogwood trees. *Grass so soft you could sleep on it. And it's beautiful there, Danny. Flowers growing from every nook and cranny. And these birds. Flocks of rainbow-colored birds. Like flying gemstones, Mama said. She called them jewelbirds."*

There was a moment of silence. Then he blinked and the boyish gleam was gone from his eye. He gave me a sheepish look.

"What . . . what was the town called?" I asked.

Jack hesitated, like he wasn't sure he wanted to part with this last detail. Like maybe it had been a secret between him and his mother. A secret protection like a kiss that no one else could see.

"Yonder," he said. "It's called Yonder."

15

June 1943

I stood frozen in place, still staring at the word carved into the tree trunk above Jack's abandoned bike. Goose bumps prickled at my skin like winter air. Jack's words from a year ago echoed in my mind. *She always promised she would take me one day.*

My fingers lifted as though pulled by marionette strings to trace the word.

YONDER.

Had it been here before? I couldn't be sure, but I didn't think so. I thought I would have noticed it, and besides, the tree skin exposed by the letters looked fresh somehow.

The longer I looked, the more certain I grew that

Jack had carved the word for me to see. He had left it above his bike, where I would be sure to find it. Which meant he hadn't drowned.

The problem was, I wasn't sure what the message meant, or why he had only left me this one word.

Yonder. Who ever heard of a place called Yonder? A place where cornstalks grew to the sky and the whole town ate together at one long table? Where there was no trouble, no war?

Who could believe in a place like that?

Before

June 1942

"It sounds more like a fairy tale, doesn't it?" I asked uncertainly. "I mean, do you really think it exists?"

Jack nodded. "I know," he said, tracing a line through the water. "I told you it would sound stupid. It's just—"

He suddenly looked up at me, eyes wide and earnest. "I see them sometimes," he said.

"See who, Jack?"

His voice dropped to little more than a whisper. But above the gentle river, his words rang out clear as bells. "The birds, Danny," he said. "The jewelbirds."

16

June 1943

A bird chirruped on the opposite bank as I walked back out onto the dock, and I saw a flash of color as it took flight. For a moment, my heart rose with it. But it was only a regular old cardinal.

Because there is no such thing as a jewelbird, I told myself.

But Jack had seemed so sincere, so sure.

Mama always said that mountain folk believed the strangest things. I remembered the tales the older scouts had told around the fire on my ill-fated camping trip. There were stories of ghostly lights that appeared along the ridges at night, which some people said were lanterns belonging to lost departed souls, always searching for a way home. Then there was the Boojum—half man, half beast—who roamed the hills and occasionally left enormous footprints along muddy tracks. Everyone knew those stories. And, of course, there were the stories we told about the Widow Wagner.

But I'd never heard of any place called Yonder, or of any rainbow birds. And Jack didn't even seem the type to believe in that kind of thing. Once I'd asked him if he'd ever seen anything odd when he delivered papers to the Widow Wagner's house, and he had only laughed.

"Danny, there's no such thing as witches. And even if there were, the widow is just a harmless old lady. The kind who knits scarves and keeps butterscotches in her pockets."

So could he really have believed in Yonder? Enough to try to find it?

Even if Jack had run away to find this magical place, he would have told me. He'd have at least left me a note—something more than a single word carved into a tree. And he never would have abandoned his dog, Winnie, to live alone with Mr. Bailey.

"He *wouldn't*," I assured myself through gritted teeth.

"Wouldn't what?"

I whirled around, nearly losing my balance.

There at the edge of the dock stood Lou. The

fingers of one hand were hooked around her overall strap, while the others curled into a fist that rested on her hip. Her toad-brown eyes studied me. Her cheeks were flushed, but then they always were, usually from either excitement or fury. It was hard to tell which just then.

"Did you follow me?" I could feel my own cheeks warming. My belly tightened like a drumskin. It had been months since we had stood this way, face-to-face. Now that we were so close, the remaining distance between us felt strange.

"So what if I did," she snapped, shaking a short lock of dirty-blond hair defiantly from her eye. "It's a free country."

I felt my body tense, waiting for what Lou would say next.

It felt like I had been waiting for a long time.

"You passed right by me," she said finally. "I was sitting on the rocks, but you didn't see me."

"Sorry," I mumbled, surprised at the sudden smallness of her voice. I shuffled from one restless foot to the other.

"You looked strange," Lou went on. "Like you were worried or something."

When I didn't say anything, she lifted her chin and looked around. "Where's Jack?"

"I don't know," I admitted.

"But you're always with him now," she said, her words bitter, like tea brewed too long.

Now it felt like something inside of me was beginning to unspool, something I had worked hard to keep tightly bundled up.

Lou opened her mouth to speak again, but before she could, I blurted out the truth. "He's missing," I said.

Lou, still openmouthed, raised her brows. "Missing?" she echoed.

"Since day before yesterday."

She took a tentative step out onto the dock, then seemed to remember herself and became more surefooted. Something about her had always reminded me of a scruffy pasture pony—the kind that might bite you if you tried to pet it—and I felt a familiar swell of affection as she plopped at the end of the dock. I sat next to her.

"Who was the last person to see him?" she asked.

"Me, I think. Unless his dad is lying."

"You think Mr. Bailey is involved?"

I shrugged. "The police don't seem to."

"So you've already been to the police? What did they say?"

"That they would take care of it," I replied. "But . . . I don't know. I don't think they took me very seriously."

Lou's eyes narrowed, but they brightened, too. She

loved nothing more than a mystery. "Well, then," she said, "we'll have to make them, won't we? And if they won't investigate, we'll do it ourselves."

And just like that, it was the two of us again. Me and the girl I had once called my best friend.

Before

September 1939

If there was anyone's soul I was sure I had the measure of, it was Lou Maguire's. Long before Jack had become my hero, Lou had been my friend.

Ever since the camping trip the summer before fourth grade, I had sat alone on the church playground during recess. After Bruce branded me a sissy, none of the other boys invited me to their games, not even the ones I used to play with. They didn't want to risk attracting his attention.

One afternoon, I was playing a lonely game of tic-tac-toe with a stick in the dirt when a rubber ball bounced in front of me. Laughter echoed across the playground, and I looked up to see Bruce Pittman and

Logan Abbot cackling along with Jeremy Pines, a squat boy who only showed up to school when there was no work to do on his father's farm.

"Hey! Chicken legs!" Bruce called. "We need a fourth for four square. Bring us the ball and come play."

Resisting the urge to squeeze my scrawny legs to my chest, I picked up the ball and obediently weaved through the girls playing hopscotch.

"I'm the king," Bruce said, pointing to his square of dirt, which had been marked by rough grooves in the ground.

"You're the jester," said Logan, pointing to the square opposite Bruce.

On our playground, the jester was the lowest position. The king was the one who got to call all the shots.

I took my place and wiped my palms against my trousers. They were already starting to sweat. I knew it had to be a trick, but what choice did I have? If I refused, Bruce would taunt me about being a crybaby until I was forced to play anyway. I would just have to do my best.

Bruce served straight to my square, and I thought I did all right to swat the ball over to Jeremy's. But before I had time to be relieved, it came spinning right back to me, twice as fast. Again, I batted it away, this time to Logan, and again, it boomeranged straight back. This time, I just barely managed to send it into Bruce's square.

"Ha!" I panted triumphantly.

"On the line," said Bruce.

"It was in your square!" I protested.

"Nope," Jeremy said. "On the line."

"Definitely on the line," confirmed Logan.

I gritted my teeth and returned to my square. Again, Bruce spiked the ball to me. No matter where I sent it, it always came flying back, harder and faster than I had hit it. I lost another round, and another. Other kids stopped their own games to watch. There was snickering behind my back.

Sweat and shame clung hot to my face as I realized that was their plan all along. There was no way out now except to keep going. To win a round. To show them all.

But I was tired, and the next time Logan jumped up and spiked the ball, it came at me too fast. I didn't even have time to move out of the way. It hit me square and hard in the face. My mouth tasted like rusty nails, so I knew that I must have a bloody lip.

"Oops," said Bruce lightly. Logan and Jeremy bent their heads to hide their snorts of laughter as Mrs. Macklenburg came bustling over, just in time to be of no use at all.

"Go to the bathroom and clean up that lip," she instructed, pulling out a handkerchief and pressing it to my mouth to stop the flow of blood. "As for the rest of you, no more four square for the week."

I stumbled off in time to hear Bruce muttering about how I'd ruined all the fun.

But I didn't go to the bathroom. I couldn't face looking at myself in the mirror. Once I rounded the corner of the church, I burst into a run and kept going until I found myself in the graveyard. I spat out a mouthful of blood and aimed a furious kick at the tombstone nearest me.

"Better be careful," Lou said, "or a ghost might follow you home."

I startled as her little head popped up from the other side of the tombstone. Mussed hair and curious green-brown eyes.

"Oh. Hi, Lou," I said, embarrassed. "I didn't see you."

"No kidding," she said, blinking at me. "Want to sit?"

I didn't have any better invitations, so I did. At least she didn't seem to care what had happened to my lip. "What are you doing out here?" I asked.

"Solving a mystery."

I looked around. "What mystery?"

She held up a book. Nancy Drew and the Clue of the Broken Locket. "Have you read it?"

"No," I said. "Those are for girls."

"You don't know what you're missing," she scoffed. "I've read almost all of them. Usually I can figure out the ending. When I grow up, I want to be a detective, too. What are you going to be?"

I stared at her blankly. I knew what other boys wanted to be. Baseball stars and policemen and ship captains.

"I don't know," I mumbled. "Maybe a doctor or something."

She pointed to my mouth. "Guess you don't mind blood, huh?"

She smiled. One of her front teeth was missing. "Doctors are okay, I guess, but I think being a detective would be more fun."

I had never noticed Lou much before, except to notice that she was odd. Now I found that I kind of liked her. "Yeah," I said. "I guess you're right."

"We could open a private-eye office," she said dreamily, "and make hundreds and hundreds of dollars."

"I guess so."

An easy silence fell over us, and for a moment the graveyard was still. I assumed Lou was lost in her daydream, and my thoughts were drifting back to the playground. The shame seeped back in.

"You shouldn't let those boys get to you," said Lou. "Especially not Bruce Pittman. He eats booger sandwiches for breakfast."

I felt my bloody lip twitching into a smile. "How do you know?" I asked.

Lou gave me a smug look. "You don't have to be

a detective to know that," she said. "Have you ever smelled his breath?"

We both burst into laughter as we heard Mrs. Macklenburg calling everyone back inside. We stood, and Lou pressed the book into my hands. "Here," she said. "I've already read this one anyway."

She skipped off ahead of me, leaving me by myself among the tombstones.

But from then on, I was never really alone again.

17

June 1943

The house was empty when I got back from the river that afternoon, still jittery with nerves from my unexpected meeting with Lou and from finding my first real clue to Jack's disappearance.

Unlike Jack, who had left me with that single word—*Yonder*—Mama had left an entire note on the kitchen table that said she had gone into the office for a few hours. She didn't return until the sky had gone soft and dark as a ripe plum. When she finally appeared, she looked dead on her feet.

She gave me a dim smile as she took off her hat. "I'm sorry I'm late, sweetheart," she said, slipping out of her shoes and sighing with relief. "I just had to do something for tomorrow's edition."

"That's okay." I was relieved that she was back, even if she did seem weary, and even if I had already decided I wouldn't tell her what I had found at the dock.

If she knew about the bike, she would worry that Jack had drowned. And she would tell the police about it. Then they would be even less interested in investigating his disappearance than they already were. But if I tried to explain about Yonder, they would either think I was out of my mind or Jack was.

"You must be starving," Mama went on, "but would it be all right if we just had sandwiches?"

I nodded, and she went to the kitchen while I picked some early tomatoes from the garden. Ten minutes later, we sat across from each other, each with a tomato and grilled cheese sandwich and potato salad Mrs. Hooper had sent home with Mama.

She looked out into the twilight as she ate. She was pale and slouched in her seat, like a flower wilting in its vase. Barely a word had left her lips since we'd sat down, and there were little creases between her brows. I wished I could read what they meant, like lines in a letter.

"Mama?"

She looked up like she was a bit surprised to see me there. "What?" she said. "Oh, I'm sorry. I was—I was thinking about something at work."

"Oh."

A muffled voice came from the living room. It sounded like Edward Murrow, who was reporting on the war from Europe. Mama must have left the radio on by accident, but she hadn't noticed. I could make out bits and pieces here and there. "Civilian losses." "Tactical maneuvers." "Troop morale."

The wafting words were a little like those ghostly lanterns some people saw bobbing along the mountain ridges at night. They meant *something*, something important probably, but it was hard to make sense of them without knowing what they were attached to. They were more frightening that way, just like the lights.

And Daddy was out there somewhere, a man made of flesh and blood lost in that forest of words.

"Do you think he'll be all right, Mama?"

"Who?" she asked. "Daddy or Jack?"

"Both."

She reached a hand down to the moon of her belly, which no longer fit under the table, like she was trying to reach into the future. "Yes, Danny," she said, after a moment. "Yes, I do. And you need to believe it, too. They need us to believe in them."

I understood what she meant. Because what is a hero without someone to believe in them?

"Mama?" I asked again.

She looked up from her plate. "Hmm?"

"Have you ever heard of a place called Yonder?"

"Yonder?" she repeated, bewildered. "Yonder isn't a place, Danny. It's a direction."

That night after supper, I took Daddy's atlas into my bedroom and scoured it for a town called Yonder. First I looked at the page for North Carolina, then Tennessee. But like Jack, Yonder was nowhere to be found.

I wondered if he had been using some kind of code. Maybe Mama was right and Yonder was a finger pointing me toward something. But what?

I reached into my bedside table for my Morse code book, but instead, my fingers fell upon a letter. Daddy had left it for me with the book before he had shipped out. He had written it out in Morse code. The first thing I had used the book to do was to decode the letter.

I'm proud of you, son, it said.

I shoved the letter back in the drawer. Would Daddy still be proud, I wondered, if he knew the secrets in *my* soul? If he knew the truth about me and Lou and why we were no longer friends?

I didn't need him there to tell me the answer.

18

That night, I dreamed I was running through a gnarled, emerald tunnel of rhododendrons. A glittering light bobbed just ahead, soft and buttery like a ball of golden yarn. Then suddenly I was pitched from the forest and into the light, and I found myself on the edge of a little town that might have been ripped from the pages of a storybook. A cobblestone lane wobbled up a hill between rows of wood houses. Clotheslines were strung up high across the narrow road, and beneath them was an endless table, with countless places laid, all awaiting a feast.

I felt a pleasant spring of recognition. I knew this place, didn't I?

But there was something wrong about the town. It was empty. My breath was the only sound. And when I looked again, the table wasn't set. The dishes were dirty, knives and forks abandoned to plates. Flies reeled around the remains of a meal that seemed to have come to an abrupt end, and the smell of spoiling meat turned my stomach.

"Hello?" I called. "Jack?"

No one answered, but as I turned in a slow circle, I noticed a flicker of movement. Lifting my gaze, I saw that perched on the nearest clothesline were five beautiful birds, bright as dragons. The sun sparkled off the shine of their colorful feathers, making them nearly too dazzling to look at. They stared at me with friendly interest.

"*Jewelbirds*," I whispered to myself.

I held out an arm, an invitation. The nearest bird began to ruffle its turquoise wings as though preparing to fly down to me.

And then a shot rang out.

The bird fell heavily to my feet. The others scattered in a haze of red and yellow and screams of fright.

I spun around in time to see Mr. Bailey scowling at me from the other side of a shotgun.

"What have you done?" I yelled.

Except it wasn't my voice. It wasn't me yelling. I

spun around again, and there was Lou. Pointing accusingly.

Only she wasn't pointing at Mr. Bailey. She was pointing at me.

19

June 1943
SUNDAY

I felt groggy on Sunday morning when my alarm clock woke me at dawn. Mama's door was still closed, so I crept down the hallway, pausing outside the bedroom that had been Jack's for a brief time.

Now, it had been invaded by a frilly bassinet, a chipped wooden rocking chair, and boxes of tiny, secondhand nightgowns. I felt a stab of resentment toward the baby who would soon wear them. The little brother or sister who made Mama so tired and who had taken the room of the big brother I had wanted.

Downstairs, I poured a heaping bowl of cornflakes and couldn't resist sprinkling them with the lightest flurry of sugar. It was Sunday, after all, and the day before me stretched endlessly into the distance, like the table from my dream. First, the paper route, followed by Sunday school, then church, then homework. At least I would have President Roosevelt's fireside chat to look forward to that night.

Fog clung to the ground as I biked toward town. The sun wasn't really up yet, so I felt like I was riding through a movie, everything painted in black and white. The morning was still and quiet, which felt a bit eerie after my dream. There was only the distant, dying hum of the night bugs in the trees, putting themselves to bed.

As I came to the peak of the hill and looked down Poplar Street, however, I saw something that made my feet pump faster.

There was a bike parked outside the *Hilltop Herald*.

My heart soared for one wonderful moment. *Jack!*

But as I got closer, I saw that the bike was too small to be Jack's. A figure sat cross-legged outside the office door. Lou. My stomach squirmed as I remembered my nightmare. I swallowed.

"Hey," I said, dismounting from my bike.

"Hey, yourself," she replied, her mouth gaping open in a lazy yawn.

I glanced around. "Um, what are you doing here?"

She shrugged. "I thought you might need some help, with Jack gone and all."

"Oh. Thanks."

I hovered while she stood and nodded to the papers. "Guess we should get going."

"Yeah. I guess so."

After I had loaded most of the papers into my saddlebags and Lou had stuffed the rest into her basket, we set off.

Even though I knew those roads like the back of my hand—had ridden them a thousand times—I felt uncertain that morning. Like the silence between Lou and me was a deep crack that had opened in the middle of the road, and the first one who spoke might just fall in.

Strange as it had been not spending time with her all these months, the silence felt stranger. Lou was never silent, even when you wished she would be.

"So," she said finally, filling me with relief, "I've been thinking."

We guided our bikes off Poplar Street and onto Magnolia Lane. Lou threw a paper toward the Macklenburgs' house but it landed on the sidewalk, only just missing the gutter. She didn't seem to notice.

"Okay," I called back. "And?" I threw a paper of my own onto the brick path in front of the Dinwiddies' house. Mr. Dinwiddie was out weeding his garden and waved.

"The way I see it, there are only three possibilities.

One: Jack ran away. Two: Jack had an accident. Or three: *foul play*."

She put extra emphasis on the last two words as she threw the next paper, which landed right at the paws of Mrs. Ballentine's collie, who would have it torn to shreds in seconds. I didn't mind much about the paper, seeing as it was Mrs. Ballentine's, but I thought with a pang of Winnie and watching Jack's father kick her back into the house.

"He wouldn't have left his dog," I said. "Not with his dad. And there was his bike. He left it by the dock. Why would he leave it if he was going to run away?"

I had told Lou about the bike the day before, but not about the word carved into the tree. I knew I should tell her, that she would take it seriously. But somehow I couldn't bring myself to. It would have felt like betraying a secret Jack had entrusted to me.

"Hmmm," Lou muttered. "You have a point there. Man's best friend and all that, right? Unless he was going somewhere he couldn't take her? Maybe he couldn't take the bike, either. He could have hopped a bus . . . or a train. Or maybe he enlisted!"

Enlisted. Sergeant Womack had said the same thing.

Even though Jack and I didn't talk much about the war, I was sure he would want to do his part. Dive into battle like he had dived into the floodwater. But he was too young.

"Even once he turns sixteen next week," I said, "he'll

need his father's permission, and Mr. Bailey would never give it. Jack told me so."

We were climbing a hill now, and the effort of getting up it while throwing papers was too great to add talking on top. For a few minutes, the only sounds were our panting and the thud of papers hitting the ground.

"Fine . . . ," Lou conceded breathlessly as we reached the top of the hill. She rested her feet against the pavement while she wiped sweat from her brow. "Then that . . . leaves two . . . possi . . . bilities. Maybe there was . . . an accident."

I gritted my teeth as I thought of the churning river. "What kind of an accident?"

"A car accident?" she mused, apparently not thinking of drowning at all. "He could have gotten hit on the way home."

"But we'd know about that by now," I said. "The police would have been called. And Dr. Penny."

"Unless there was a cover-up!"

"A cover-up? Come on, Lou. This is Foggy Gap we're talking about."

I remembered, though, the feeling I had whenever I passed by the Musgraves' old farm or Mrs. Ballentine on the street—that I didn't know my own town half as well as I'd thought. I didn't know the things we were capable of.

But a cover-up wouldn't explain the carving in the tree.

"Well, that just leaves one option," said Lou. "Foul play."

I could tell by the way she said it, like she was a character on one of Mama's radio soap operas, that she didn't really believe it.

We rumbled onto a wooden bridge that crossed over a clear little stream, flashes of mossy forest on each side. Fog still rose off the water. Jack had called that kind of river fog "a poor man's rain." We ducked to pass under the willow that grew in a crooked arch over the bridge.

"I'm out of papers," Lou called, and I pulled over next to her to hand her some more to stuff in her basket. As I did, I glanced down and saw a familiar word catch my eye from one of the front-page headlines. I peered closer.

WARSAW GHETTO REPORTED WIPED OUT BY NAZI FORCE, blared the headline.

So that's why I had seen the name *Warsaw* on Mama's desk. I felt a tightening in my chest. I looked away from the paper.

"We'll have to go back to the police and see what they've found out," Lou was saying. "Maybe they'll share their investigation notes with us."

Annoyance twanged through me, like the strum of an out-of-tune banjo. Lou never changed. That was the best thing about her, and also the problem. She was still the girl in the graveyard dreaming of being Nancy Drew.

I stood on my pedals, launching myself forward. "Come on," I snapped, without quite knowing why I felt so rotten all of a sudden. "Otherwise I'll be late for Sunday school."

I flew by the last few places, deliberately staying just ahead of Lou, until only the Widow Wagner's house remained. Then I had to slow my pace to get up the hill.

"I'm trying to help, you know," Lou retorted. I could almost hear her nostrils flaring. She had caught up with me by then, and she pumped her feet until her legs were a blur, speeding past me. "I thought you might appreciate it after what—"

I steeled myself for what she would say next. But as we summitted the hill, Lou slammed on her brakes, and I nearly crashed into her.

Then she screamed.

Before

August 1941

"What is it?" I called down from the window. "Why are you hollering?"

My post-Sunday-fried-chicken-lunch stupor had been interrupted by Lou shouting my name up at my window.

"You'll see," she said. "Come on. We have to go to my house right now!"

I groaned. By then, Lou and I had been friends long enough for me to know that she wasn't going to leave me to my nap. She had that starry gleam in her eyes that meant trouble. Usually the fun kind.

"Gimme a minute," I said.

Together we biked over to the Maguire place, a white farmhouse that needed a fresh coat of paint. It was nestled against a half-moon hemlock stand on one side, with horses grazing in an overgrown pasture on the other. Cutting across the pasture was a stream, with a little stream house where the Maguires kept their milk and butter and meat cool in the summer.

From the way Lou had been carrying on, I expected a traveling circus to have pitched up in her front yard. But it was the same old dozy house, baking like a cake in the August heat.

"Lou, what are we doing?" I asked, slumping over my handlebars. Mrs. Maguire made the best lemonade, and I could have sorely used a glass.

"We've got a case," said Lou triumphantly. "The Case of the Silver Rattle."

"The what?"

"There's this baby rattle," she explained, abandoning her bike right in the middle of the driveway. "Granny ordered it when George was born. There was a little cup and spoon, too. Solid silver. Really, really expensive, get it?"

"All right . . ."

"Well, each of us kids used them as babies. And Ma just got them back out for the new baby."

Mrs. Maguire had just had her fourth baby, Charlie, a few weeks before. Mama had taken me over to meet him. Charlie slept in Mrs. Maguire's arms the whole time, but Jimmy (who had been the youngest until

Charlie) kept trying to squirm onto Mrs. Maguire's lap until finally he stomped off in a huff.

"Why does a baby need a solid silver rattle anyway?" I asked.

Lou shook her head, befuddled. "Who knows? Anyway, she had them all laid out to be polished this morning. The rattle, the cup, the spoon. And then poof." She snapped her fingers. "Gone."

"That's the big mystery?" I asked. "That's what you woke me up for? Lou, she probably just forgot where she put them."

Lou grinned. "No," she said. "They were stolen. And I have proof."

She ran toward the hemlock stand, beckoning for me to follow. The stand was sparse, with a soft blanket of hemlock needles to cover the ground and muffle your footsteps, and beams of sunlight that lit up craggy, crouching rocks. But a little farther in, the trees closed ranks, darkening the forest into a cave.

Lou bounded to the far edge of the trees and pointed to the ground. "There!" she said triumphantly.

I crouched down to see. A little silver spoon lay there, half-buried by hemlock needles. "You found this here?"

"Yup," said Lou. "By accident this morning. And that's not all. Whoever stole it left a trail."

She gestured toward the shadowy forest beyond. I could see a very narrow path that cut through the sprigs of joe-pye weed and leafy carpet of galax that covered the ground.

"That? It looks more like a deer trail to me," I said.

"No. The thief obviously ran away through there. They probably didn't notice dropping the spoon, or they were in too much of a hurry to care."

"Maybe," I said, unconvinced.

"Come on," Lou urged. "Let's follow it and see where it leads."

And because I didn't really believe there was a thief waiting between the dark trees, his pockets full of baby silver, the idea of trying to catch him sounded like it could be fun. "All right, then," I said. "Let's go."

We had to walk single file, with Lou swinging a stick in front of us to knock down spiderwebs. I knew she and little Jimmy weren't strictly allowed to go this way. Their land ended where the hemlocks did, and these woods meandered on up endlessly into the hills, where a grown man could easily lose his way. But I reasoned that Mrs. Maguire was busy with the baby, and we would stick to the trail—or whatever it was.

Pretty soon I looked back and couldn't see any light from the way we'd come. It was too quiet for a forest. Where were all the chattering birds and the squirrels rustling in the treetops? All I could hear was the far-off sound of the river. And the path seemed—if it was possible—to be getting narrower.

"Nobody could have come this way," I said, as branches clawed at my arms. "We should go back."

But Lou forged on. "I can see something up ahead—a clearing."

Looking over her shoulder, I could see it, too. A place where the path widened, and it wasn't so dark. We had almost reached it when suddenly a figure stepped out right in front of us, leaving just enough light for us to see her face.

Gaunt and hunched, the Widow Wagner stood in front of us, her silver hair braided in a crown around her head, her eyes wide and wild. I only just had time to register that she had a flower tucked behind one ear and a raven perched on the opposite shoulder before her arm reached out as if to take hold of me. She opened her mouth as though to say something, but a horrible scream spilled out.

We ran.

It was only as we were hotfooting it back through the forest, to the safety of the Maguire house, that I realized it hadn't been the widow who had screamed at all. It had been the raven.

20

June 1943

Now the Widow Wagner stood in front of us once more, her mouth frozen open in a gasp. Lou had nearly run into her as she'd crested the hill.

I had never forgotten the way the widow looked that day in the forest, reaching out. And though a jealous Jimmy had confessed later that afternoon to stealing "his" rattle and things so the baby couldn't take them ("I should have known . . . the culprit is always right under the detective's nose," Lou groaned), it didn't make the widow any less suspicious. What had she been doing there, wandering the inky-black forest with only a raven for company?

The widow had changed greatly since I had last

seen her. She was wearing pink slippers and a blue-and-white knit blanket over her stooped shoulders. Her thinning gray hair was tied back with a ribbon, like a girl's, but a few strands had managed to escape and hung limply around her face. Her skin was very pale with a greenish tinge, the color of healthy sapling wood just beneath the bark. But there was nothing healthy looking about her. She seemed frazzled and confused and looked nervously over her shoulder at her house, as though there was something she didn't want us to see.

I followed her gaze, remembering Bruce's talk of German prisoners of war hiding out there. But there was no sign of anything out of place. One of the rocking chairs on the front porch seemed to sway just slightly, but no more than the breeze might have moved it.

Then I felt Lou's elbow in my ribs. She was staring at the side of the house. A word had been painted there in huge, dripping red letters.

KRAUT

Kraut was a word I started to hear after we entered the war. Kraut as in sauerkraut. It was a dirty word for a German. The enemy.

I felt sorry for the widow then. She didn't seem like

a witch, not with her frail form and her proud blue house with those letters like bloody gashes across it. She seemed like a scared old lady. I smelled the faint whiff of butterscotch.

But then I glanced at the paper in my hand again. The words *NAZI FORCE* glared up at me. And I remembered that we were at war, and in war, there are sides. A right one and a wrong one.

"Here you go," I said, holding the paper out stiffly. "Come on, Lou."

Lou was still staring at the widow as she took the paper. "But—"

"Come *on*, Lou," I said again.

Just before I turned my back on the widow, I saw the black beat of wings as a raven came to land on her porch. As I biked away, I heard the bird caw. A scolding, maybe. Or a threat.

21

Lou caught up with me again at the bottom of the hill.

"Who do you think did it?" she asked breathlessly, her brain already whirring faster than her feet.

"I don't know," I said. "But it's true, isn't it?"

She huffed as we rattled back over the bridge. "Just because she's from Germany doesn't mean she wants them to win the war."

My fingers squeezed the bike brakes, and I came to a stop in the middle of the bridge. "Do you know what's happening over there, Lou?" I asked sharply. "Do you understand what the Nazis are doing?"

For once, words seemed to fail her. She shook her head.

The truth was, I didn't understand it, either. Not really. It was like something I had glimpsed through a keyhole. I had seen just enough to know I wasn't sure I wanted to see anymore.

There had been news articles from places like the *New Republic* magazine laid out across Mama's desk. Screaming headlines about massacres.

Stray words whispered between my parents just before Daddy left for war. *Terrible. Unthinkable. Evil.*

And just once, a phrase on the radio before Mama turned it down. *The reported extermination campaign . . .*

And yet, no one ever really *said* anything. President Roosevelt had never mentioned it in his fireside chats. Mrs. Pattershaw never said anything at school. Pastor Douglass hadn't even mentioned it in his sermons, and he loved talking about evil.

I could almost convince myself I had imagined that there was anything else happening besides the fighting, which was bad enough. But then I would hear another whisper. See another headline. And I would know that something else *was* happening. Something involving ghettos and camps and death. Something that meant this was a war unlike any other.

"All you need to know is it's really bad," I said to Lou. This much I was certain was true. "And I didn't see an American flag hanging in the widow's window, did you? Everyone has to pick a side now. Either you fight for good, or you're on the side of evil."

I felt the truth of my own words sweep through me, and I sat up tall on my bike seat. Just then I thought I could have taken on a whole battalion of Germans, were they to start parachuting down from the sky. *Courage when it counted.*

Then I saw how Lou's face had crumpled. I knew she was thinking of her brother, and I remembered the ugly words Bruce and Logan had used to describe him. *Coward.*

"Lou, I'm sorry. I didn't mean—"

"Don't worry about it, Danny," she said, her words stinging. "I have to go anyway."

Without another word, she started off. She would turn right to get home, and I would turn left.

"See you at church?" I called, hoping I had misunderstood the venom in her voice.

She looked over her shoulder. Her eyes glistened. "We don't go to church anymore," she said. "Not since George. People stare. It's too hard for Ma."

"Oh, right," I said, but she had already disappeared into the bright morning.

Before

October 1942

Sunlight splashed across the river as Jack dived into the water, still in his clothes. Even though it was autumn, the afternoon was hot as July. It was a bit like the five-dollar bill Granny Mabel sent me every birthday, which always arrived a few weeks late. A belated gift from summer.

And Jack meant to use it wisely. He had shown up at the house earlier that day and told me to get my swimming trunks on. "No way am I gonna let another year pass with you not knowing how to dive," he said. "And don't try to pretend. I see how you always jump in feetfirst."

I explained that Daddy had tried to teach me every summer since I was five. My brain knew what I needed

{ 167 }

to do, but my body just wouldn't do it. My feet wouldn't let me plunge headfirst into the water, so I always ended up on my belly. It was just one more thing that made me different from the other boys. Weaker.

But Jack wouldn't listen, and half an hour later, there we were.

When he emerged, shaking the water from his hair, he held a narrow rubber inner tube flat against the surface of the water.

"Now, remember . . . aim for the inside of the circle," he said, squinting up to where I stood at the end of the dock. "Imagine all the water outside the circle is concrete. You want to hit your head on concrete?"

"No," I said, my toes scrunching up against the boards.

"Arms up and knees bent," Jack instructed. "That's it. Let your arms lead the way. One, two, three!"

The first eight times we tried, I flopped face-first into the water.

"It's useless," I said. "Let's just try to catch some fish."

"Naw," Jack said, still paddling in place in his sopping undershirt. "You'll get it, Danny. Just keep your chin tucked this time. Diving is all about trusting yourself. Easy as that."

He must have seen my soggy, skeptical look, because he laughed. "Well, if you can't trust yourself, then you trust me. Nothing bad is going to happen if you dive into that water, all right?"

I remembered the feeling I had driving home from the beach years ago, when I hadn't mustered the courage to follow Mama out past the shallows.

I didn't want to feel that way again. So, shivering, I pulled myself back onto the dock. I took a deep breath and concentrated on what Jack told me. I kept my head down.

And this time, when I splashed into the water, it was headfirst.

When I came back up, Jack was whooping and clapping.

"Did I do it?" I gasped.

"Sort of," Jack said, laughing. "A few more tries, and you'll have it."

And he was right. That was the day I learned how to dive.

Afterward, we sat barefoot on the dock, fishing lines bobbing in the water. My skin felt warm, and I wasn't sure if it was from the sun or from the pride I felt lighting me from within.

"Thanks," I said. "For teaching me, I mean."

Jack had taught me lots of things since we'd started spending afternoons together. How to string a fishing line, and which kinds of rocks were likely hiding crawdaddies underneath. How to tell the time of day just by looking at the sun.

I had taught him a few things, too. Sometimes, he would bring his math workbook and I would show him how to solve a problem. He would cross his ankles and let his knees fall into his elbows, furrowing his brow with concentration as I did the sums. Then he would try while I watched. Sometimes when he got a problem right, he would bang his heel against the dock and holler out in triumph.

The problem was, I wasn't nearly as good a teacher as Jack. And mostly, he got the answers wrong.

We weren't thinking about sums that afternoon, though. Jack winked at me as he reeled in his line to recast it. "You did good. Everybody should know how to dive. Just in case."

We sat in silence, listening to the river and waiting for the trout to bite.

"Were you scared?" I asked finally. "When you dived in to save the Coombs twins?"

Jack shot me a surprised look, and I thought he might not answer me. I had learned by then that Jack was like an oak leaf in summer. Most of the time, you couldn't see past his quiet, breezy exterior. But if you could catch the light at just the right angle, he would be illuminated and you could glimpse inside, see how he was put together.

The light must have been right that day, because Jack answered me after all. "I wasn't scared," he said. "I just saw them floating there and figured I could help. Knew I had to try, at least."

"Everyone else was too scared," I said. "Mr. Pittman sure was." And then, after a moment: "I guess you're not like other people, huh, Jack?"

Jack raised a quizzical eyebrow.

"You're not scared of anything," I explained. "Not fights or floods."

He gave me a strange half smile. "I'm afraid of plenty," he said. "Just maybe not the same things as everybody else."

"Like what?"

Jack stared at me another moment before his line began to move. He pulled it out of the water to reveal a rainbow trout. Small, but big enough for him to take home for supper.

As he bent forward to unhook it from the line, his shirt lifted, and I saw a nasty bruise running up and down his side.

I gasped.

At the sound, he turned and saw me staring.

I didn't need to ask what happened. I knew from the wincing look he gave me and from the way he had kept his shirt on while we were swimming so I wouldn't see. This was his father's doing.

Before I could say anything, Jack spoke.

"Never mind, Danny," he said, tugging his shirt back

down. The light had shifted, and my glimpse behind his facade was over. "Just never mind."

So I didn't say another word about the bruises. Not that time. Not any other time.

And I never asked what Jack was afraid of again.

22

June 1943

By the time I got home from my route that Sunday morning, I was in a terrible mood. And I had no one to blame for it but myself. Who did I think I was, saying what I had to Lou about choosing sides? Maybe Jack knew more about being afraid than I had realized, but that didn't mean I knew any more about bravery.

I felt like I had lost Lou all over again.

Mama had just laid a stack of flapjacks on the kitchen table when I trudged through the door, feeling heavy and useless as an old boot that's lost its mate. She announced she was too tired to go to church that morning, which was a small mercy. I didn't need

Pastor Douglass to make me feel like more of a sinner than I already did.

"I was going to ask if there was any sign of Jack," Mama said, "but I'm not sure I need to."

I shook my head and slid into my seat. With some difficulty, Mama maneuvered herself into the chair across from me and passed me the maple syrup.

"How about I put something in the paper this week?" she asked. "Maybe someone will have information and come forward."

I straightened, about to tell her that was a great idea, when she went on.

"But, Danny . . ." She bit down on her knuckle, like she did when she was deep in thought, or the baby was making her feel sick. "A boy like Jack—who's had to face everything he's had to . . . I think we have to consider the possibility that he ran away. That maybe he's better off wherever he's gone. I don't want you to be crushed if we don't find him."

I stabbed at my breakfast, deliberately making my plate shriek with the sound of my fork hitting it. "You don't know him like I do," I said. "*Nobody* knows him like I do."

Which was true, wasn't it? Maybe I didn't know everything about Jack, but I knew more than anyone else. *I* was the one who had spent all those mornings on the paper route and afternoons at the dock with him. It was me he'd confided in about his father, his mother, and about Yonder. And now it felt like I was the only one who believed in him. His only shot at being found.

"You've been a wonderful friend to Jack," Mama said slowly. "But . . . that boy has been through quite a lot. There might be things he didn't share with you. Things we don't know. Things he didn't want to talk about."

I thought of the bruise snaking up his side, his fingers rushing to tug his shirt back down.

"Maybe he wouldn't have had to go through so much if we had done more!" I cried, letting my fork clatter to my plate. I knew I was pushing it, knew if Daddy was here he'd send me to my room for speaking to Mama this way.

But when she looked up at me after a long moment of silence, her eyes were shining. "I can't argue with that, Danny."

23

Since we didn't have to go to church that morning, I had a few free hours, and I needed to get out of the house. I wanted to escape the thoughts that had suddenly taken over my head, like soldiers in an invading army.

I wanted to believe that Jack had been trying to tell me something in code. That *Yonder* was the key he had left for me. So that I might follow him through whatever door had swallowed him up.

But I still didn't understand why, even if Jack had set off to find Yonder, he wouldn't have just told me. He had trusted me enough to tell me about Yonder in the first place, after all. And if he hadn't gone to find the town, what was the carving supposed to mean?

I decided to go out looking for scrap metal. I was behind on my collection, and I figured that if I couldn't get any further in my investigation to find Jack, at least I could make myself useful.

I had already combed the house for anything metal we didn't need, and a few things we did. I had emptied Daddy's tool chest of most of his nails and screws, and even the head of a hammer I had never seen him use. By the time he would be back to notice their absence, I hoped, the war would have been won and he would know I was only doing my part to help us to victory.

Mama had let me have the last of her aluminum foil, some old pots and spoons, a handful of bobby pins, and a few tin boxes she used to keep old letters in. And I had donated Mrs. Hooper's tin cowboys, of course.

The rest of my collection was mostly things I had found on the side of the road, by the river, or in the woods. Bottle caps and fishing hooks and bits of old barbed wire. Even foil gum wrappers. Twice, I had found tire rims just rusting away in the shade of the forest.

The town was still quiet as I wound through the streets. Most everyone would be at church. To get my mind off Jack, I let my imagination drift off to the ceremony where the scrap-metal contest winner would be announced in front of everyone. The kid who had done the most out of anybody in town to help us win the war. I could almost feel the medal being placed around my neck.

I was just bending down to pick up a bottle cap when I realized that I had stopped outside of the Prices' house. And that Dylan Price was sitting in his tree swing, watching me. The gold star in the window behind him almost looked like it was perched on his shoulder.

"Hi, Dylan," I said. Even from here I could see his eyes were red.

"Hi, Danny."

Dylan had always been quiet. He sometimes tucked comic books into his textbook and read them secretly during class. We had never been friends, but he had never joined in with Bruce's teasing, either.

"Scrap-metal competition," I said in explanation, holding up the cap.

"I haven't collected any," he replied, his voice flat. "Mrs. Pattershaw will be mad."

"She won't," I assured him.

My gaze was pulled again to the stitched gold star. It was like a sunset, impossible not to stare at, even though it hurt your eyes. "I'm really sorry," I said. "About your dad."

He didn't say anything.

"Well, I'd better go," I said quietly.

It took everything I had to bike off slowly instead

of racing away from that house, and the thought that it could have just as easily been Dylan saying sorry to me. My house with the gold star in the window.

When I came to the bridge where Lou and I had argued earlier in the day, I decided to leave my bike behind and look around in the woods. I had no desire to pass the Widow Wagner's house again.

I kept my eyes on the ground, searching between the mossy rocks, looking for anything that didn't belong to the forest. My heart leaped when I discovered an old tin can abandoned at the roots of a red oak tree.

Jack had pointed out a red oak the morning we'd found our Christmas tree. He said there was nowhere better to search for a turkey than beneath the boughs of a red oak. Apparently, it was a good place to look for bean cans, too.

After that, though, my luck ran out. I searched for a long time without finding so much as a staple. My mouth felt dry, and I was drawn toward the sound of the nearby stream. I knelt in the rocks beside it and cupped the cold water in my hands, slurping up as much as I could.

When I'd had my fill, I wiped my mouth with my wrist, stood and turned.

That was when I saw the bird.

24

The bird was perched on a nearby birch sapling and not much bigger than a sparrow. Its head was covered in red feathers that bled into orange, then gave way to bright turquoise plumage.

My first thought was that it was some kind of parrot. Perhaps the circus had come to Asheville and this bird had escaped. Only I would have known if the circus had come, because there would've been ads in the paper. Half the town would've driven to see the animals unloaded from the train cars, the elephants marching right through the streets.

If it wasn't from the circus, where could a bird like this have come from?

Flocks of rainbow-colored birds. Like flying gem-stones.

That's how Jack said his mother had described them. The birds that lived in Yonder. The jewelbirds.

I see them sometimes, I heard him say.

Suddenly, the bird ruffled its feathers and took flight again, heading into the forest. Before I knew what I was doing, I tore off behind it.

In that moment I would have given anything to trade my chicken legs for bird's wings.

I can't remember what I thought as I darted through the woods, trying to keep up with the bird. Perhaps that it was another sign from Jack. That he had found Yonder after all, and he sent a jewelbird to bring me there, too.

It couldn't be a coincidence. The very bird that Jack had described to me appearing as my hopes of finding him were fading.

It was like the bird was playing a game with me, flying just deep enough into the murky forest that I thought I had lost it, then alighting onto a branch long enough for me to spot it again.

I followed it into a valley of ferns, sending ripples through the sea of green fronds. Panting, I raced after it, tripping over a decaying log and regaining my footing in time to see bright wings flapping between two hazel trees. As I reached the crest of the hill, the bird fluttered into a maze of mountain laurels. I took off after it and soon found myself lost in the mossy shadows and tangled pockets of thicket.

Just when I had given up hope of finding the bird, I spotted its wings again. The red of them against the gloom of the forest was like the spark of a match being lit in the dark.

Again, I followed as it flew away from the web of laurels and out into open woodland, where the trees soared into the sky and gray boulders huddled like sleeping giants.

Dropping my hands to my knees, I looked up at the rock where the bird had perched. It stared down at me and blinked.

Wait for me, I wanted to shout. *Take me to Jack!*

But it was only a bird. And in the next instant it had taken flight once more, swooping through the ancient trees until they had swallowed it up, wings and all.

This time I had lost the bird for good. I kicked the dirt hard with disappointment.

I hadn't only lost the bird. I had lost my first real chance of finding Jack, too.

25

June 1943
MONDAY

The next morning, my thoughts were still with that bright bird that had slipped into the forest. And I wasn't the only one whose thoughts were elsewhere. In Mrs. Pattershaw's class, legs were already jiggling under desks with anticipation of the summer break, just around the corner.

I kept chancing glances at Lou, trying to signal I was sorry for what I had said the day before, but she gazed past me out the window. Her eyes looked flat, like shallow puddles, the skin beneath them smudged with shadow.

Lou would never go to war like her brother, but the war had marked her just the same. It had marked

Dylan Price, too. Really it had marked all of us in our own ways. It was thousands of miles away and yet there with us, all the time, like an unforgiving sun.

Mama and I had stayed up the night before, listening to President Roosevelt give one of his fireside chats. I was hoping he might explain what exactly was happening in Warsaw. Answer some of the questions about the war that had begun to form in my mind. Instead, he talked about the coal miners' strikes, which had been happening on and off for months, and how important the supply of coal was to the war effort. So I had gone to bed none the wiser about Yonder *or* the war.

At lunch hour, I jostled along with everyone else to get out of the classroom. By the time I spilled into the hall, Lou had disappeared. She wasn't in the cafeteria, either, so I thought perhaps she had gone home for lunch.

I finished my sandwich and, not wanting to spend any more time sitting alone in the cafeteria, headed back toward Mrs. Pattershaw's class. I would wait in the hallway until it was time for class again.

The hallways were mostly empty as I retraced my steps back. As I rounded the corner I nearly ran smack into Bruce and Logan.

"Hey, watch where you're going," said Logan. He held a bulging lunch bag, clenching it hard.

Bruce turned on his heel to find me staring at him. A slick smile spread over his face. "Well, hey there, Danny boy."

I dropped my gaze. And it was then that I solved a mystery that, of all the mysteries prowling my mind, I least expected to solve.

There on Bruce's shiny penny loafers were three drops of red.

26

I looked away from Bruce's shoes, not wanting him to realize what I had seen.

Before either of us had decided what to do next, we heard the smart *tappity tap, tappity tap* of Mrs. Patter-shaw's shoes.

"Eager to get back to class, I see," she said. "I had no idea you were so fond of spelling, Logan."

I hid a smile. The only word Logan could probably spell right was his own name.

"Come on, then," she said, ushering us in as the bell rang.

I made a beeline for my desk and glanced toward the door every time I heard footsteps approaching, hoping to make eye contact with Lou. Could I find a way to get her to look at the droplets on Bruce's shoes? Proof, surely, that he had been the one who had painted that slur in red on the Widow Wagner's house. Maybe a clue like that would be enough to make her forget that she was mad at me.

Kids shuffled through the door, laughing at a last joke or yawning ("Cover your mouth, please, Annie," scolded Mrs. Pattershaw). There was the normal buzz of lunchtime conversations winding down, like cicadas at dusk. But then I realized that there was something else, too. An undercurrent, like a far-off river. Whispers being passed between the kids.

I felt myself stiffen. Was there news I hadn't heard? Had someone spotted the black army car crawling through town? If so, whose house was it calling on? Who had already lost their father or brother and didn't know it yet?

Lou ambled in after everyone else. She cradled a book under her arm and wore the same far-off expression she had all day.

Then, as she reached her desk, she stopped dead.

"Lou, take your seat now, please," Mrs. Pattershaw instructed. "We're already late to start our lesson."

But Lou didn't take her seat. She stared down at it, and slowly plucked something off it.

A feather.

Before

December 1942

It was a frigid cold morning, and I was glad to be done with my route. I blew warm air into my gloves once I'd thrown my last newspaper, then started in the direction of school.

Halfway there, I heard a car coming up behind me and looked over my shoulder to see Mr. Pittman's brand-new truck. To my horror, it began to slow.

The passenger-side window rolled down, and Bruce stuck his freckled face out.

"Brrrr," he said, exaggerating a shiver as the fresh air hit him. "I'd offer you a ride, but looks like there's no room." He gestured to the truck bed, which was filled with freshly cut fir trees. Every Christmas, the Pittmans

made a big show of chopping them down and bringing them to all the businesses in town.

When I didn't answer, Bruce continued. "Maybe you want someone to walk with you?"

"No," I said quickly. "That's okay."

He snorted. "Like I would."

"Now, Bruce," Mr. Pittman cautioned, a lazy half warning.

"Don't worry, Dad," Bruce replied. "Danny and I are friends now. Aren't we, Danny?"

I gulped and looked away from Bruce's knowing smirk.

"Hey, Danny," came Jack's voice from behind me.

He slowed to an easy stop and tipped his head at Bruce and Mr. Pittman. It was impossible to miss the twin scowls that fell across their faces.

"Jack," said Mr. Pittman flatly. A greeting, I supposed. "We'd better get on now, Bruce. Don't want to be late. I'd hate for you to get in trouble."

He gave us a smug, pointed look.

Then the truck was pulling away, headed down the road. Even after it had disappeared, I felt a sinking feeling, like I was biking through quicksand. I wondered if Jack had heard anything.

"We'd better watch out," he said. "They're liable to have thrown down nails to give us flat tires."

I mustered a small laugh. "You're late today," I said.

It had been a year since Jack had stayed with us, and almost as long since we had started our route together. He always used to beat me to school, but these days it seemed like he took longer and longer.

"Just taking my time," he said, as we started off again.

I thought that was a bit strange, since on a morning so cold, even school had to beat being outside. Yet somehow, Jack's cheeks weren't chapped and red like mine, though his coat was nowhere near as warm. At least he was wearing a new scarf, along with the mittens Mama had given him.

As the school came into sight, we heard the first morning bell ring and biked faster. By the time we arrived, almost all the kids had funneled in. Only a few were left walking up the front steps.

One of them was Lou.

She looked small, holding her books close and shuffling up the steps.

"Poor kid," Jack said, nodding his head in her direction.

"What do you mean?"

"I saw the article about her brother."

"The article?" I asked, head shooting up in surprise.

"In the paper this morning. Said he was court-martialed a couple weeks back. For desertion. They reckon his unit got sent up to the front line and he got too scared and bolted. Some cook turned him in."

I couldn't think of what to say. I didn't know George Maguire well, but he was Lou's favorite brother, and he'd always been kind to me. He had been a hard worker on their farm and one of the first boys from Foggy Gap to enlist.

Now he was going to go to prison for desertion. And the whole town knew.

"You really didn't know?" Jack asked.

"No. Anyway, since when do you read the paper?"

"I like to look sometimes," he said, sounding a bit hurt, "same as anybody."

"All right, sure."

"Anyhow, people are going to say a lot of things about George Maguire they got no right to," Jack said, his voice heavy with something like regret. "You might want to look out for Lou. That's all."

"Sure thing," I said. "I will."

The lie melted right off my tongue like butter, but it sure left a sour taste behind.

27

June 1943

I gazed across the room at Lou, my jaw slack. My first thought when I saw the feather in her hand was of the jewelbird I had seen the day before. But the feather she held wasn't bright and shining. It was the color of oatmeal. Looking closer at her chair, I could see that it was covered in feathers. Some tan, others black or white.

Then the clucking started. It was coming from Logan. Bruce joined in next, making another noise, without hardly moving his mouth.

"Bawk," he cooed. "Bawk, bawk, bawk."

A chicken. He was trying to sound like a chicken. I remembered the bag Logan had been holding before class. Logan, whose father had won the poultry competition at the county fair five years running.

Then I realized something even worse. It wasn't just Bruce and Logan who were making the chicken noises. They were coming from every corner of the classroom. My gaze darted around. A few people's eyes were round with surprise. Others, like Dylan, were looking down at their desk. But some were giggling, and many had joined in.

"What on earth—" Mrs. Pattershaw started. She was the only one in the class who wasn't staring at Lou, hadn't figured out what was happening yet. "Everyone, quiet down, please."

The noise kept building.

All that time, Lou had been staring at the feather in her hand. Then she tore her eyes away from it. And, finally, she made eye contact with me.

She looked not at me but *to* me. Her eyes shone.

Jack had told me to look out for her.

I gripped my desk with both hands to keep them from covering my ears. I didn't want to hear the riot of clucking anymore.

Stop! shouted a voice inside of me. *Just STOP it! Can't you see what you're doing? Can't you see it's wrong?*

But who was the voice speaking to? My clucking classmates? Or me?

I willed myself to get up, but it was as if I could already feel Bruce's hands pushing me back down, like they had so many times. Like they'd done at the dugout on the day I first met Jack. And like they'd done one horrible day in the graveyard last winter—a day I had done my best to forget but probably never would.

So I only stared back at her, wide-eyed and silent.

"Quiet!" shouted Mrs. Pattershaw now, her cheeks red and flustered. "You will stop this instant or you'll all be here until nightfall. And for heaven's sake, Lou Maguire, *sit down*!"

Lou looked at Bruce. I don't know what she saw in his face, but the next instant she was swooping toward him like a specter raised by all that clucking. Her hands twisted into talons like she meant to scratch his eyes out.

As she lunged at him, he turned to protect his face, and I saw that it was pale and round as a fearful moon. He, too, had transformed, all that pride and certainty becoming pure terror.

The next second, Lou had descended on Bruce, tugging his hair and scratching at his face, aiming kicks for his shins.

"Get off me!" he cried. "Someone get her off me!"

"My . . . brother . . . is no . . . coward!" Lou yelled. "And neither am I!"

Mrs. Pattershaw was yelling, too, as she tried to

separate Lou from Bruce, and the room filled with the sound of every chair scraping against the floor as people moved to get a closer look. The door banged open, and someone rushed in.

Together, Mrs. Pattershaw and Mr. Bunch finally managed to haul Lou off Bruce, who looked like he had been in a fight with a holly tree.

"You come with me, young lady," Mr. Bunch said, steering Lou to the door by her shoulders. "Never have I seen a such a shameless show of—"

"Mr. Bunch," piped up Mrs. Pattershaw, her voice shaking as she followed them, "I do believe she was provoked. I should have seen—"

Mr. Bunch put up a hand. The class, at last, was silent.

"There is no excuse," he said. His cheeks were ablaze with anger. "*No excuse.* Get that boy to the nurse to clean him up. I'll phone his father from my office."

With a final bang, he slammed the door behind himself and Lou. It was all over. The battle was done, and nobody, it seemed, had won. We had lost it, every single one of us.

28

Mrs. Pattershaw was too shaken to teach us much that afternoon. Instead, she asked us to write an essay on why our behavior was wrong.

I sat numbly over my blank paper as the time dragged on, thinking about how Lou had looked at me before she'd gone for Bruce. She had wanted my help and I had been too afraid. I hadn't had courage when it counted.

In the end, I only managed to write one sentence.

It was my fault.

As soon as the afternoon bell rang, I ran to the first floor. I hoped that I could peek through the secretary's window and glimpse Lou in Mr. Bunch's office.

But there she was, sitting on the bench in the hallway, her knees tucked up under her chin.

I wove between the high school students, too busy with their gossip to notice me, and sat down beside Lou.

She didn't move a muscle.

"I brought you this," I said, passing the blue *Nancy Drew* book over. She'd left it by her desk.

She unknotted her arms and snatched it back.

"I'm sorry," I said, "about what happened in there."

"Are you, Danny?" she said, looking up at me. "Are you sorry?"

"I *am* sorry, Lou," I replied. "You don't know how sorry."

"Then why'd you do it?" she asked fiercely. "Why did you stop being my friend after the news about George?"

I searched my brain for the right answer.

"Maybe I just don't know how to be a very good friend," I said.

Lou scoffed and pointed up toward our classroom. "Obviously not."

We sat in silence for a minute. My cheeks burned.

"Some things you're born knowing, but other things you have to work at," Lou said finally. The hallway had emptied out, and it was just us. Her voice was quiet, the edges of her words not so sharp.

"Maybe . . . maybe I can work a little harder at being a good friend?" I asked.

"Maybe so." Her chin was dimpling the way it always did when she was feeling stubborn. She wasn't ready to be won over so easy.

And that made me want to smile. Lou hadn't been broken by Bruce, or her brother, or me. She was stronger than that.

"Why are you out here, anyway?" I asked.

Lou shrugged. "When Mr. Bunch brought me here, Mrs. Miravelle was waiting outside the office. She said there was something that needed his urgent attention. He went in, and I haven't seen him since."

At that instant, the door to the office burst open and Mr. Pittman marched out, red-faced and huffing.

I braced myself. Surely there was no way Mr. Pittman could have heard about the fight and gotten to school in the time it took for Mr. Bunch to march Lou down to the office?

I was ready for him to give Lou a piece of his mind. But he barely spared us a glance. Instead, he slammed the door behind him, marched straight past our bench and toward the front doors.

Then we heard low voices from Mr. Bunch's office. Voices that sounded like they didn't want to be overheard. Lou and I stared at each other. Then, together, we crept to the door, leaning in to listen.

"Appreciate your understanding," said a man's voice. It was familiar, but I couldn't place it.

Another voice, this one familiar, too, spoke then. "John Bailey's been through enough. I'd like to protect him from this mess. So of course, nobody can find out."

I felt Lou's fingernails dig into my arm. The voices were talking about Jack's father.

"I understand," came Mr. Bunch's voice. "Though I must admit, I don't agree. But you'll know best."

Then there was the sound of rustling, like men getting to their feet, and Lou and I scrambled back just as the door opened. Officer Sawyer stepped out, Sergeant Womack right behind him.

Officer Sawyer spotted us and stiffened. Sergeant Womack didn't see us right away. His pox scars were white against the red of his cheeks.

"Hello, Danny," said Officer Sawyer, tipping his hat at me.

I wondered if he had noticed how my hands were clenched into fists.

Mr. Bunch followed the police officers, his weary expression falling on Lou. "I suppose I still have to deal with you," he muttered. He seemed to be talking more to himself, though. "Should have mentioned something to Mr. Pittman while he was here but . . .

perhaps it was for the best I didn't. I'll be back shortly for you."

"We'll leave you to it, then," Sergeant Womack said to Mr. Bunch. "Now that this matter has been, ah, resolved."

Mr. Bunch nodded, pinching the skin between his eyebrows. "Good afternoon, gentlemen."

As the police officers turned to go, I took a step toward them.

"Sergeant?"

Sergeant Womack stopped, reluctantly turning on his heel.

"Is there news about Jack?" I asked. "It's just . . . I thought I heard you say the name Bailey."

His face betrayed nothing. "Did you now?" he drawled. "How strange. I'm afraid I don't have any news for you. Boys that age, well, they run away all the time, and we can't waste all our resources finding someone who doesn't want to be found. Now, unfortunately, I'm in a bit of a hurry. If you'll excuse me."

Rage rose like a river inside me as Sergeant Womack walked away. He had lied straight to my face.

Officer Sawyer started to follow, but I reached out for his arm. I had already let Lou down today. I didn't intend on letting Jack down, too. He stopped like he had expected it, turned and grimaced. His hat was too big and fell down almost to his eyebrows.

"Please," I murmured. "I know he's lying."

Officer Sawyer glanced over his shoulder as Sergeant Womack disappeared through the front doors.

"I see you kids like detective mysteries, huh?" he said, gesturing to Lou's book. "That explains a lot."

Lou gripped the book protectively. "So what if we do?"

"Well, you'll know then that there are things police officers aren't allowed to say," he said. "And I probably shouldn't even say this much, but . . ."

He flicked his eyes once in each direction, making sure nobody was coming. "What is it?" I asked, steeling myself. "I can handle it."

"It's just . . . ," he started, "It would be better if you go back to thinking about other things. You're just a kid. It's almost summer. You should be fixin' on getting into some trouble. Not looking for Jack Bailey."

"What's that supposed to mean?" Lou snapped.

"Have you even talked to Mr. Bailey?" I asked. "Searched his house? Or did you not even bother? Are you too busy *protecting* him instead?"

Officer Sawyer flinched, then drew up straighter in his neatly pressed uniform. "Just you take my word for it," he said. "I've already said too much."

"You haven't said anything!" I nearly shouted. "And I'm not going to stop looking for him. I won't!"

Officer Sawyer sucked in a long breath. "Let it go,

Danny," he said, teeth gritted. "It would be the best thing for everyone if you just let. It. Go."

And without another word, he turned and followed Sergeant Womack out the door.

Lou shook her head. Her cropped hair seemed to stand on end, like she'd been struck by lightning. "I'll tell you something, Danny Timmons," she said. "This stinks. It stinks like a cover-up. What are they protecting John Bailey from that no one else can know about?"

"We can't let them get away with it, Lou." I dropped my voice. My anger had stiffened into resolve. "And I know what I need to do. But I'm going to need your help."

29

After I left school, I pedaled into town like a tornado was on my heels. I had to get to the *Herald* office and tell Mama what I had overheard. Lou and I had our own plan, but maybe Mama could help, too. Maybe get a detective from Asheville, or even Charlotte, to come investigate.

Why had I given up on Mr. Bailey as a suspect so quickly? I had seen the carving in the tree and wanted to believe it was a message from Jack, telling me he was all right. But what if I had been wrong, and he'd done the carving some other time? Maybe I just hadn't noticed it before.

And the bird—well, perhaps it was just a strange

coincidence. Was it possible that I had wanted to believe Jack was all right so badly that I had simply imagined it? I wasn't sure.

All I knew was that the police were hiding something to protect John Bailey, and I was going to find out what.

I was reaching for the handle of the *Herald* door when it flew open, and Mr. Maynard came billowing out like a storm cloud, nearly knocking me over.

"Well," he said, by way of apology, "maybe *you* can talk some sense into that mother of yours."

"I don't—I don't know what you mean, Mr. Maynard," I stumbled.

He waved me off. "The front page no less," he muttered under his breath as he huffed his way to his car.

Utterly confused, I walked into the office. Mama was sitting at Daddy's old desk in the back corner, looking very pale, and Mrs. Hooper was buzzing around her in a frantic kind of way.

"He really shouldn't speak to people that way," Mrs. Hooper said. "After all, you were trying to do the right thing."

Even Mr. Ogletree had stirred himself from his usual afternoon nap to come and sit on the desk opposite Mama's, where he was shaking his head glumly. "What an age," he grumbled. "I hardly know what to believe anymore myself."

"Are you all right, Pearl?" Mrs. Hooper asked.

"You're looking a bit ashen."

"I'm fine," Mama said. "Just need some water, that's all."

Then she caught sight of me. "Oh . . . Danny!"

"What's going on, Mama? What was Mr. Maynard so upset about?"

"Nothing," Mama said, but she didn't sound like herself. Her voice was high and wispy, like she was talking in her sleep. "It was nothing. Everything is fine. Let me just get that drink of water."

"I'll get it," said Mrs. Hooper, who was frowning now.

But it was too late. Mama heaved herself up from her chair. She stood for a second, then her eyelids fluttered.

The next thing I knew, she had collapsed on the ground, and by the time Mr. Ogletree began shouting instructions I was already sprinting out the door to get Dr. Penny.

Before

January 1943

"Take care of your mama, okay, Danny?"

Daddy whispered the words in my ear, and I knew that was because Mama would have scoffed and said it was her job to take care of me. "Take care of her, and the baby, when it comes. I'm counting on you, all right?"

"All right, Daddy," I said. "Until you come home."

"Until I come home."

He gave me one last squeeze, and then he was pulling away, taking with him the familiar smell of ink and Ivory soap. He wore an easy smile on his clean-shaven face, and there was nothing urgent in his voice. But one hand was in his pocket, jangling the change he kept there in a way he only did when he was anxious.

Next to us, Mama was sniffling and pretending not to. A few yards away, a woman dissolved into a fit of sobs as a young man—her son, probably—boarded the bus in front of us. The bus that would take all the men away to Camp Croft, where the army would train them. From there, they would go to war.

I knew not all of them would come back. Already, there were four fresh graves in our church's graveyard. And on Christmas Eve, we had stopped on our way to church, hats in our hands as we listened to a distant trumpet playing taps as another solider was unloaded off the train in a coffin.

Not Daddy, *I told myself sternly.* Not Daddy, with his broad shoulders and swift stride and barking laugh. Not Daddy, who I loved.

"You okay?" *Jack asked, as Daddy and Mama embraced.*

"I—" I started. But I couldn't finish, because the truth was I wasn't, and I didn't know how to pretend I was. "I'm glad you're here," I said instead.

Daddy had insisted Jack come for the send-off breakfast Mama had fixed, and then to the station with us. Now I wondered if it was so that the car wouldn't feel too empty on the way home, with just Mama and me.

Daddy clapped Jack on the shoulder and murmured

something in his ear. Jack closed his eyes a moment, nodding his reply.

"Thank you, Mr. Timmons," he said softly. "For everything."

"Hey, no long faces now," Daddy said, holding out his arms and shooting us one last smile. "I'll be back before you know it."

Then he picked up his suitcase, boarded the bus. He waved as it pulled away, while those of us left behind cheered or clapped or cried. Only when it had trundled off out of sight did I see a tear escape from Mama's eye.

I wanted to cry, too. But then I looked at Jack, who was staring at me. He gave me a small smile and a nod. I did my best to smile back.

So I swallowed my tears. "It's all right, Mama," I said, wrapping my arms around her. "We're going to be all right."

30

June 1943

I paced the hall outside Mama's room while Dr. Penny
was with her. When he finally came out, I stood up
straight and balled my fists, trying to prepare myself
for the worst.

"Just a case of low blood pressure," he confided,
squeezing my shoulder reassuringly. "Truly, Danny,
there's no need to worry about her, or the baby. She's
just run herself ragged. I've put her on bed rest until,
well, the time arrives, but that's just a precaution."

I let out the breath I'd been holding in, but guilt
gnawed away at my relief almost instantly, sinking
into me like rats' teeth.

I had noticed Mama looking tired for days. Why

hadn't I said anything? Done anything? Why hadn't I kept my word to Daddy?

"Do you have anyone who can come and stay?" Dr. Penny asked. "Someone to help?"

Mrs. Musgrave would have helped us, but she was gone.

"My granny is coming," I said, "but not for another week."

"Well, it will be up to you to look after her until then," he replied. "Make sure she gets as much rest as possible. Do you think you can handle that?"

I had never so much as looked after a kitten before, let alone my own mother. But I said I could.

I spent the next hour bumbling around the kitchen, floating from the ice box to the pantry and Mama's recipe box, trying to find something I could understand how to make. I had started with grand visions of pre-rationing red velvet cakes and fried chicken, but everything had so many steps and ingredients, and in the end I had settled for warming up some soup.

If Mama was disappointed, she hid it well.

"Mmmm," she said, smiling as I entered the room and set the tray down in front of her. "Chicken noodle. Just what the doctor ordered."

She was lying in bed where Dr. Penny had left her an hour before. I watched her closely as she pulled the tray up to balance on her belly and began to eat.

The color in her face had come back a bit, but she still looked tired and frayed. She glanced at me and raised her eyebrows.

"There's no need to stare at me like I'm a bomb that might go off," she chided, "even if I might be shaped like one." She patted the bed next to her.

"So you're really all right?" I asked, sitting down.

"Fit as a fiddle," Mama replied. "Though I could just about die of embarrassment, fainting like that. Like some grand Victorian lady. Heavens."

"Dr. Penny says you have to stay in bed."

"So I heard. I suppose I won't be returning to the paper any time soon. That'll leave Mr. Ogletree in charge, Lord help us. Not that Mr. Maynard will mind much."

That last bit made me remember how Mr. Maynard had come barreling out of the *Herald* that afternoon, and how Mrs. Hooper had complained about the way he'd spoken to Mama.

"What exactly happened before you fainted?" I asked. "Why was Mr. Maynard so angry at you?"

A sigh filled up Mama's chest like a sail, and she let it rest there a moment before she breathed it out. "Are you sure you want to know the truth?"

"I'm sure."

She sipped her soup, then swirled the spoon around the bowl a few times. "Well, it's a bit of a long story," she said. "This winter, some of the national papers and magazines ran articles about a report. A report that spells out something the Nazis are trying to do."

"To win the war, you mean?"

Mama shook her head. "That's just it, sweetheart," she said. "It's not to win the war. It's something much worse."

I felt a jolt, like hands shaking me awake from a dream I didn't want to leave. What could be worse—*much* worse—than war? Mama paused, giving me a chance to tell her that I'd accidentally left the stove on or the milk out and should really get back downstairs.

But I didn't. So she went on. "You see, for quite some time, Hitler has been trying to convince the Germans that they would be better off without some people. Even before the war, the Nazis began taking away their rights. Then their businesses, and then their homes. And now, they are putting them into camps."

I swallowed. "Camps?"

"Extermination camps," said Mama gently, still watching me closely. "The Germans are killing them, Danny. Old men and women, young children, and everyone in-between."

My heart gave a sickening lurch. Mama's face was very still, just the way it had been when we'd said goodbye to Daddy.

"Children?" I forced myself to say.

"*Jewish* children, Danny. Along with their families and with others Hitler has stoked prejudice against. He's already killed millions, it seems. With millions more still in the camps. Millions of people that could be saved."

My mouth had gone dry as cotton. *Millions.* I had pieced some of this together from headlines and whispers. But millions of people? Killed for simply being Jewish?

Though I hadn't met many Jewish people before, besides a few of the shopkeepers in Asheville, I understood that some people spoke unfairly about them, even called them rude names. I thought it was just more small-mindedness.

There was *nothing* small, though, about what Mama was saying now.

"But . . . but why?"

Mama gazed at me intently and shook her head. "There's never a just reason," she said. "Not to hate people the way the Nazis do. I suppose some people embrace that hatred because if they believe someone else is lesser, then they must be superior—noble, even."

"They aren't *noble*," I said in disgust.

"No. They certainly are not. What they are is angry, and Hitler gave them a cause to channel their anger into. He knew many Germans would be all too willing to make Jewish people the scapegoats for everything wrong in Germany. He blamed them, you see, for all of the country's problems, then offered to 'fix' those problems with this terrible plan. Your daddy has been listening on the shortwave for years as Hitler has spilled his poison. Getting his followers to focus on their anger and their fear and their prejudice so much that somewhere along the way, they stopped thinking of the Jews and the others as people at all."

A chill shook me, and I felt I might go on shivering for a long time.

"It's evil, Mama," I said. "*He's* evil."

Mama didn't speak for a moment. "Evil is only as powerful as we let it be," she said finally. "But I'm afraid that Hitler and the Nazis have fed the flames. They've made it very, very powerful."

"But why doesn't everyone know?" I asked. "Why don't they talk about it on the radio?"

Mama leaned forward to brush the hair from my eyes. "If you only knew how often I've asked the same questions," she said. "But it brings me back to the argument with Mr. Maynard. Your father decided to publish a small article about the report in the winter, before he left. Mr. Maynard wasn't happy about it. And there was more news last month. A Jewish revolt in Warsaw. People fighting for their lives though they must have known they could never win."

"And they didn't," I said, thinking of the headline

I had read in the paper the day before. WARSAW GHETTO REPORTED WIPED OUT BY NAZI FORCE. "It's over now, isn't it?"

"That's just it, Danny. It's not over if the world can take a lesson from how bravely they fought," Mama replied, squeezing my hand. "How bravely people all over Europe are still fighting. That's why I published the articles about it. I hoped it might inspire others to see what's really at stake in this war. Until people see it there in front of them, it won't be real to them. They need to read it from their papers, hear it from their radios."

"So then why was Mr. Maynard upset?"

She grimaced. "Well, the same reason we *don't* hear about it on the radio or see much in the papers, I suppose. Some people—the very people who decide what we know about the war—don't want to believe it. Perhaps the idea of something so terrible happening is too hard for some people to accept. Other people might believe, but they don't think it's worth reporting on."

"Not worth reporting on?" I echoed.

"People like Mr. Maynard think the camps are not our problem—that we should keep our focus on winning the war. It's easy for some people to think that way when it's all happening overseas. If they don't see an injustice, then they don't have to take a stand, you see? If it's happening to somebody else, then maybe you can convince yourself that it couldn't happen to you, so it's not your battle to fight. But that's exactly the kind of thinking that led to the terrible things happening in Germany. Some people simply don't understand what we're fighting for in this war. It's not just land, or democracy, or sovereignty, Danny. It's our *humanity*."

"But . . . ," I started, staring down at the bright checkerboard of Mama's quilt, "but that kind of thing . . . it couldn't happen *here*. Could it?"

Mama closed her eyes. "No one could have imagined it would happen in Germany," she said quietly. And then: "Even here, there are those who agree with Hitler, or at least some of his thoughts. And—"

She opened her eyes and turned her gaze toward the window.

"What, Mama?" I asked gently.

"Danny, prejudice is like . . . like a germ, or a virus," she said. "Nobody is immune. That sickness—that *evil*—it can take many forms. In Germany, it created those camps. Here, it created segregation, and slavery before that."

She turned to look at me then, took my hand and squeezed. "I can't tell you that this kind of thing can't happen here, sweetheart, because, well, it already has. It still does. Just look at the Musgraves. If this town were free from prejudice, they would still be here."

I opened my mouth to ask my next question, but just then, Mama gave a little gasp, making my heart leap. "Mama? Are you all right?"

To my surprise, she took my hand and brought it to rest on the crown of her belly. Before I had time to get embarrassed and pull it away, I felt a hard thump against my palm. I gasped, too.

"Was that—"

"The baby," finished Mama. "I've never felt it quite so hard."

A tiny fist—or maybe a foot—knocked into my hand again. It was hard to believe that something so small could push so hard, be so insistent. It lightened the weight I felt pressing down on me a little.

Still, worry rattled in my chest as I wondered just what kind of world that baby was going to be born into.

I left Mama after that, without asking any more questions. Dr. Penny had said she needed rest. Besides, I had some thinking of my own to do.

I felt as though the world had once been a smooth egg that I could cradle neatly in my palm. But I had squeezed too hard, and cracks had begun to form. Now what had been there all along, invisible beneath the surface, was beginning to spill out.

Images flashed through my mind. Blurry faces of

crying children and falling snow. Lou rushing at Bruce Pittman. George Maguire running away from battle. Mama and Mr. Maynard arguing. Jack falling through the door of the *Herald* that December night, black-eyed and broken-ribbed, needing our help.

Somehow, everything felt connected by threads as strong and fine as spider's silk. I just didn't understand how.

There was another image, too, that rose to the surface. One I couldn't shake.

It was Mrs. Musgrave's face on the day, nearly three months ago now, when she came to tell Mama she was leaving.

Before

March 1943

Once Daddy left for the war, Mrs. Musgrave started coming over even more than before. She often brought with her a basket of corn muffins or a mason jar stuffed with daffodils. Sometimes I would come home from school to find the parlor door closed, the smell of something fresh out of the oven wafting in the air, and I would know that she had stopped by for a visit.

One Saturday, she brought Jordan over, and the two of them helped Mama and me to make our own victory garden. I was in charge of digging up the grass where the garden bed would go.

I had rarely held a shovel before, and Mrs. Musgrave took it from my hands after my first few attempts at digging.

"It takes some getting used to," she said.

She demonstrated the right way to step on the shovel head while Jordan suppressed a giggle, showing off the front tooth he had just lost. Fortunately, soon after that I unearthed an old rusty horseshoe, which quickly took his attention off my shoveling abilities.

"My daddy is signing up for the war, too," he told me proudly that afternoon, while the two of us were digging holes in the earth for the seeds Mama had bought from the general store. "And he's going to win."

"Hush now," Mrs. Musgrave said. "He's doing no such thing."

I flashed Jordan a secret thumbs-up anyway, which was rewarded with another gap-toothed grin.

When we were done planting, Jordan and I were sent to the kitchen to fetch endless watering cans.

"Seeds are thirsty things," Mrs. Musgrave explained. "Keep them watered, and before long you'll have all the squash and tomatoes you can eat. And besides all that, there's nothing better than watching the things you planted grow."

I knew that all this—the garden, the extra visits— was Mrs. Musgrave's way of keeping an eye on Mama, which made me grateful to her.

And maybe it was because I was so grateful that Mama had a friend to talk to that I overlooked the way their conversations changed as winter gave way to spring. The sound of their voices became a low, urgent hum of words, the kind of noise that warns you from treading too near a beehive.

Just as Mrs. Musgrave seemed to be keeping her eye on Mama after Daddy left, Jack kept a close watch on me. As the weather warmed, we spent more time down by the river. We talked less, though, and when we did, it was usually about fishing or baseball. Ted Williams had enlisted in the navy, and other players were sure to follow. (Even when you weren't talking about the war, somehow you still were.)

I didn't mention Jack's father or Yonder, and he didn't mention Lou or Bruce. And that seemed to suit both of us just fine. Sometimes, I thought about asking him what Daddy had whispered in his ear the day Daddy had shipped off, but I knew my father would say it was none of my business.

Jack never asked me if I was all right with Daddy being gone, but I figured just hanging around with me was his way of making sure I was. It was another thing that didn't need talking about, but I did want Jack to know how much I appreciated it. So I started making him come for dinner as often as I could convince him.

One afternoon, when we'd been particularly successful at hunting crawdaddies, I got Jack to come home with me so Mama could boil them into a stew.

When we got home, the parlor door was closed, so I knew Mama and Mrs. Musgrave must be inside. But that day, they weren't quiet at all.

"This can't be the end of it," Mama was saying. The urgency in her voice sent prickles up my spine. "There must be someone who can step in."

"There's nobody," came Mrs. Musgrave's voice. It trembled with something I had never heard in her words before: anger. "Nobody will step in. Who would side with us over Nick Pittman?"

"I do!"

"But you don't have a say in who gets loans and who doesn't. Nick Pittman has the bank in his pocket."

"We'll go to the bank again," Mama said. "This time, I'll tell them—"

"It wouldn't change anything," Mrs. Musgrave said, frustrated. "He's got too much power. He's got the whole town."

There was a long pause.

"And you won't stay?" Mama asked.

"And be sharecroppers on our own land?"

"No," said Mama, defeated. "I suppose not."

Then came the sound of one of them blowing her nose and the murmuring of voices, like the two women had suddenly moved close together.

When I glanced at Jack, his brow was set in a deep furrow.

"I don't understand," I whispered. "What's Mr. Pittman done?"

"It sounds like he's gotten the bank to deny the Musgraves their loan," Jack said. "Farmers have to get one every year. Without it, they can't buy what they need to sow their crops. And without crops, they can't afford to live."

"But why would he do that?" I asked, thinking of the heaping crates of produce Mrs. Musgrave and Jordan brought us week after week. "Their farm produces more than most of the others around here."

"Exactly," Jack muttered.

I was about to ask what he meant when the answer rapped me on the head.

"You mean he got the bank to deny the loan so he could take the land for himself? But . . . he can't get away with that. It's got to be against the law."

Before Jack could reply, Mama spoke again.

"Where will you go?"

"Pittsburgh," said Mrs. Musgrave. "My sister lives there. She says there's good factory jobs. A good school for Jordan."

A knot had formed in my stomach. Pittsburgh? I couldn't imagine the Musgraves in a city like Pittsburgh. They belonged on the farm that had belonged to them for over eighty years, where they could watch the things they planted grow.

"And you don't want to wait a little longer? To make sure there's nothing that can be done?"

I heard Mrs. Musgrave sigh. It was a small sound, all the sadder for its smallness.

"Pittman's made up his mind," she said. "And once that man decides he wants something, nobody in this town's going to convince him otherwise. Most of them wouldn't even try."

Just as I realized the voices sounded closer than they had before, the door opened and Mrs. Musgrave stood there, blinking at me and Jack. Mama bustled up behind her, stopping short when she saw us.

"We weren't eavesdropping," I said. "We just—"

"It's all right," Mama said. "This way you can say goodbye."

Mrs. Musgrave nodded at Jack, who had gone white and still as if he had been turned to ice. I didn't understand why. As far as I knew, he'd only met Mrs. Musgrave a few times.

"Goodbye, Danny," Mrs. Musgrave said solemnly. "You take care of that garden and mind your mama."

"Yes, Mrs. Musgrave," I replied. "Please tell Jordan I say hello—or, I mean, goodbye."

Her eyes were red, but she raised her chin as she made her way toward the door. I remembered what she had said to me about Bruce years before. "Don't give him your tears. That's letting him win."

She was taking her own advice. Mr. Pittman wouldn't win anything more from her than what he'd already stolen.

Mrs. Musgrave paused at the door, smoothing her blue dress and taking a breath before opening it. Then she walked out, Mama following behind her.

And that was the last we saw of Daphne Musgrave.

31

June 1943
TUESDAY

I awoke with a start the next morning to find the wind coming through my open window, the smell of dew blowing in with it. The world seeping in.

My conversation with Mama came rushing back to me. Everything she had said about the camps across the sea, about people not wanting to believe what was happening in them, and about prejudice being like a virus.

I can't tell you that this kind of thing can't happen here, sweetheart, because, well, it already has. It still does. Just look at the Musgraves. If this town were free from prejudice, they would still be here.

Mama's words had made me understand something

that should already have been obvious: the reason why no one would stop Mr. Pittman from stealing one of the best farms in town. It was something I felt sure they'd never let him do to the Abbots—Logan's family—or even the Maguires. It was the same reason Mrs. Ballentine could keep Jordan from setting foot in the library and nobody said a word. And the reason most people in town called the Musgraves by their Christian names instead of their last names.

It was prejudice, plain and simple. Not just the prejudice of a single heart, but of a whole town, like Mrs. Musgrave had said. And the more folks who shared it, the less anybody would question it, the more powerful it became.

What had happened to the Musgraves wasn't the same as what was happening in Germany, but the force behind it was. Those events were gossamer strands in the same terrible web, invisible to most people, except the ones caught inside it, and the few on the outside, like Mama, who made an effort to see.

I felt slow and heavy as I got up and got dressed, like I had molasses running through my veins.

As I passed by Mama's room, I opened the door just a crack. She was still sleeping, her face smooth and peaceful. Gently, I closed the door and tiptoed down the stairs. When I went out to get the milk, I found a basket of muffins and biscuits at the door with a card from Mrs. Hooper at the *Herald*. I took one of the muffins as I set out, leaving the rest on the kitchen counter for Mama.

It was a gray morning—the kind that threatened to turn into a gray day—and the sky was dotted with white mist, like a dappled pony.

When I arrived at the *Herald* office, I unrolled the paper at the top of the stack and quickly scanned it to see if Mama had been able to write an article about Jack's disappearance. But there was nothing there—she must not have gotten the chance before she'd fallen ill.

Hopefully it wouldn't matter. Hopefully between us, Lou and I could solve the case ourselves. My stomach squirmed as I remembered the plan we had made the day before.

I had the sudden feeling that today was the day Jack's case would break wide open. And if I could find a way to bring him back—if I could put that one thing right—then it felt like there was a chance that everything else could somehow be put right, too.

As I rushed through my route, whizzing by all the familiar houses, I imagined the people inside—the women who brought Bundt cakes to church picnics and the men who volunteered at the firehouse—and wondered what they had thought when they'd read the articles about the extermination camps and the

Warsaw revolt. Had their eyes simply brushed past the headlines and moved on to read about the prices of meat? I wondered what they thought about the Musgraves leaving town. Did they know what Mr. Pittman had done? Did they think it was right?

The whole town looked different to me that morning, though it didn't feel like Foggy Gap had changed so much as I had. It was like returning to a favorite bedtime book Mama used to read me, only to find that that there were holes in the story, and the ending made no sense.

By the time I reached the Widow Wagner's house, I wasn't so sure that any of us had the right to judge her. And someone, it seemed, agreed with me. The side of her house had been painted over, the graffiti wiped clean.

32

When I finished my route, I took a deep breath and, instead of heading for school, I pedaled toward the place where Lou and I had agreed to meet, at the bottom of the road to the Baileys' house. She was waiting for me there. We hid our bikes behind a patch of mountain laurel and ducked into the woods.

"So what did Mr. Bunch say yesterday?" I asked, once we were safely tucked away. "About you beating Bruce up?"

Lou smiled at the memory. "He suspended me," she said lightly, picking a piece of grass to chew on. "For the rest of the school year."

Which wasn't quite as bad as it sounded, since it

was our last week of school. And since we'd already been planning on skipping today anyhow.

"What did your parents say?"

The smile dropped from her face. "Ma wasn't even very mad when she read Mr. Bunch's letter," she replied. "She just went kind of blank. But I'm not allowed to tell Daddy. She doesn't want to upset him. So I have to pretend I'm sick. I snuck out from my bedroom. It's nice in a way . . . since Ma doesn't want him to know, she can't punish me too bad."

Lou shrugged, but she chewed harder on her grass and kicked at the dirt beneath her saddle shoes like she wished it were Bruce's backside. "Bet Bruce's mother is bringing him breakfast in bed right about now," she muttered.

"Booger sandwiches?"

Lou rewarded me with another little smile. "Extra slimy."

The morning had grown darker instead of lighter as it wore on. Rain was coming, no question.

"Well, guess we should get going," I said. No time like the present to stage a break-in. And besides, I wasn't sure how much longer my nerves would hold.

"Speaking of the Pittmans," Lou said as we crept through the underbrush, "I've been wondering . . . why do you think Mr. Pittman was at the school yesterday? Mr. Bunch might have made a report to the police about Jack not coming to school, so that explains why he might be meeting with them. But why Mr. Pittman?"

I bristled at the sound of Mr. Pittman's name. If I never heard it again, it would be too soon. But Lou had a point.

"I bet he's in on it somehow," I said. "He's hated Jack ever since Jack saved the Coombs twins and made him look like a coward."

Lou scrunched her face up in thought, then shook her head. "But if he's in on the cover-up, he wouldn't have stormed off like that. It seemed like whatever the police were saying, he didn't like it."

My brows stitched together as we climbed. "Well, there's no way Mr. Pittman was there to stand *up* for Jack."

"Maybe he was there for some other reason. Maybe Bruce is in trouble with the law," Lou replied wistfully.

I let out a short burst of laughter. "I bet you're right!"

Lou gave me a disbelieving look.

"I saw red paint," I explained, ferns tickling my ankles. "On Bruce's shoe. Red like the paint on the Widow Wagner's house the other morning."

Her eyes widened. "The Pittmans just got done painting their barn again," she said. "Ma mentioned it at dinner the other night. How they're always painting things that don't need a fresh coat just to prove they can. They probably have buckets and buckets of red paint lying around. And besides, who else in Foggy Gap would do a thing like that?"

"That must be it, then. Maybe we'll get lucky and Bruce will be arrested."

Lou shushed me, pointing ahead. I hadn't realized how close we were to the Baileys' cabin. It squatted just ahead now, looking about as welcoming as a snake's nest. One we were about to walk straight into.

If the police were protecting Mr. Bailey from an investigation, we needed to know why. And there was nowhere better to start looking for answers.

"You stay here," I said, when we had reached the edge of the house's little clearing. "I'll go around back. We can keep watch for a while to make sure he's not in there. We need some kind of code so we can say if we see—"

"Or," said Lou, "we could just do this." She looked at the ground and found a rock the size of a robin's egg.

Before I could stop her, Lou was sprinting forward, taking cover behind Mr. Bailey's old truck. Then she launched the rock from her hand and it hit the tin roof with a loud *thwack!*

I gasped, fighting the urge to run. My hands had gone all clammy. From inside, Winnie began to bark. I waited to hear Mr. Bailey yelling at her to shut up, but the voice didn't come. The longer Winnie's barking went on, the more sure I felt that Mr. Bailey wasn't inside.

I inched forward from my hiding spot to meet Lou.

"I don't think he's in there," I said. "He wouldn't let Winnie keep barking like that."

"Then now's our chance."

Lou stood and, with one final glance in each direction, scuttled up to the house. She looked back at me. "What are you waiting for?"

She was right. We couldn't afford to wait any longer. Not when Mr. Bailey might return at any moment. *Courage when it counted*, I reminded myself.

I unfolded myself from behind the rusting truck and ran to the porch.

"What if the door's—" I started.

"Locked?"

She had already turned the handle, which shrieked on its hinges but opened wide in welcome.

I couldn't help but think there was nowhere in the world I wanted to be less.

33

Winnie came barreling out onto the porch, her tail wagging so fast it was nothing more than a blur, her paws scrabbling at my legs.

"Hey there, girl," I said, bending down to stroke her coarse tawny hair and let her lick my face between squeals of excitement. I did the best I could to calm her, worried that Mr. Bailey could be somewhere close enough to hear.

"We'd better get her back inside," said Lou. She stepped into the cabin and clapped her hands. Winnie darted after her. I followed them and closed the door behind me.

The smell was impossible to ignore. Sour and sharp,

like something rotting, and beneath that the unmis-takable whiff of mildew.

"Pee-yew!" Lou said. I could see her waving her hand in front of her nose, but only barely because it was so dark in there. The windows were covered with burlap sacks that had been cut open and laid flat. I moved to the nearest window and lifted up the make-shift curtain, hooking it back on one of the nails above that held it in place.

The window was open, so a fresh breeze wafted in with the light. Blinking, Lou and I each turned in a slow circle, taking everything in while Winnie wove figure eights around our feet.

At first glance, there wasn't much to see. We were standing in a room with two narrow beds, one against each wall, and two dressers in the nearest corners. Beyond that, there was a kitchen with a little wood-stove and pots and pans hanging from the ceiling. Between the kitchen and the beds was a table and three chairs. One of the chairs had been knocked over and lay curled up on its side like a wounded animal. I wondered if Mrs. Bailey had been the last person to sit in it. It certainly didn't look like the Baileys had done much entertaining recently. I certainly hadn't ever been invited inside—and hadn't ever wanted to be, truth be told.

There were shelves in the kitchen for plates and

bowls, but they were empty. Stacks of dishes were strewn around on the countertop, and spilled out of the tub that must have counted as the sink. Half-eaten portions of unidentifiable meals were congealing in some of them. Which explained the smell.

The bed nearest to me was a tangle of gray sheets. A muddy sock peeked out from underneath it. The dresser top was littered with objects that looked like they'd been thrown there at random. A dull hunting knife, a chipped mug, an empty tin of chewing tobacco, its lid gaping open and a few coins and bits of twine inside.

"What a pigsty," Lou muttered, wrinkling her nose.

But the other side of the room was neat as a pin. The bed was covered with a frayed quilt made up of triangles of blue, burgundy, and cream. The kind of quilt someone had long ago stitched with love. I ran my fingers over it. Winnie hopped onto the foot of the bed and gave a little sigh as she curled up there. The way she settled herself so easily made me think that it was her usual spot. Clearly, this was Jack's side of the room.

On his dresser was an ancient baseball mitt with a ball nestled tenderly inside, like a child tucked into bed. Stacked beside that were a few schoolbooks and papers, which Lou began to rifle through.

"See anything odd? Anything out of place?"

"I don't know," I replied. "I've never been here before."

The truth was, the whole house gave me a terrible feeling. I didn't like imagining Jack here, sharing this little space with a man like Mr. Bailey. It felt like imagining him living in a tiger pen. How had he done it for all these years?

"These are all just normal school things," Lou said, looking down at the stack of papers like they had offended her. "Jack wasn't doing too good in math, huh?"

"No," I said, remembering suddenly that I still hadn't worked out what the deal was he had made with Mr. Bunch just before he went missing.

"I don't see any signs of a fight. I'll check under the bed. You look through his dresser. I don't want to see his underwear."

"Shouldn't one of us stand guard or something?" I shot a nervous look out the window.

"We'll be quick," Lou said, sliding down onto her belly and peering under the bed. "Yuck, these shoes smell. Wait . . . what's this?"

She pulled an old shoebox from beneath the bed. Glancing out the window once more, I crouched down next to her. The box was mostly filled with papers. There were a few old school things in there—report cards and tests, things like that. A Christmas card to Jack that I realized with a pang had been sent by

Mama last year. Lou was leafing through them when I spied something gold at the bottom of the box.

"What's that?"

Lou pulled out a large gold star, with a smaller silver star at its center, attached to a striped ribbon. "Is it some kind of award?"

"No," I said, taking it carefully from her. It was heavy in my hands. "It's a military medal. My uncle got one kind of like this. But Daddy keeps it behind a glass case in his office."

"*Mr. Bailey?*" Lou asked. "A war hero?"

"I knew that he fought," I said. "But Jack never told me . . ."

Before that moment, I'd been certain that if there was one thing Mr. Bailey was not, it was a hero. Only a bully would treat a child the way he treated his own son. And yet, here was his medal. The kind only heroes got.

I remembered Jack telling me what a good man his father had been before the war. Secretly, I had wondered if maybe that was another story his mother had told him. Maybe she thought it would be kinder to let Jack believe that his father had once been something better.

I had never believed it might be true until that moment, holding the medal.

But if Mr. Bailey had really been a good man—a

hero—what had happened?

Jack's voice came to me again.

The war happened. It got under his skin, like some kind of spell.

"Well, it's still not a clue," said Lou, shaking me back to the present. "Did you look in his dresser?"

"Not yet."

"Well, hurry up!" she scolded. "Mr. Bailey could be back any minute."

"I know," I grumbled. "That's why I said there should be a lookout."

"Fine, I'll do it. You just keep searching."

It had gotten darker still as the storm rolled closer. I opened the top drawer of the dresser reluctantly, feeling strange about going through another boy's clothes. I ignored the socks and underwear and went to the next drawer. It was mostly empty. There were a few shirts—including the ones Mama had given him two Christmases ago—some long johns, overalls, and trousers. And the navy-and-white-checkered scarf he'd started wearing last winter, which I figured had probably been donated to him by the church. The scarf reminded me of something, but I couldn't put my finger on what it was.

In the corner of the drawer was an item that obviously didn't belong with all the other things. Something soft and pink. Gently, I reached in and picked it up.

The cloth unrolled into an apron. It was dotted with grease stains and burn marks, and had been patched up here and there with loose stitches, clearly done by a clumsy hand. Certainly not the same hand that had sewn Jack's quilt.

I had a sudden image of Jack sitting up late at night, darning his dead mother's apron, and I felt wrong for having gone through his things. I quickly balled the apron back up and returned it to the drawer.

Then I moved over to the stack of papers Lou had been going through and picked up one that looked older than the rest. It was Jack's birth certificate. The yellowing paper listed his name, his birthday, his parents' names, and his place of birth.

I read it once, and then again.

My heart stuttered in my chest.

There must have been some kind of mistake.

"Danny!" Lou said, shaking my shoulder. "Mr. Bailey is back!"

I whipped around to see a figure trudging up the road to the house, eyes on his feet. Still far enough that we might just be able to tiptoe out the door without him seeing, if he kept his head down.

"We have to go," Lou said, and for the first time I could hear fear in her voice. "Right now, Danny!"

I nodded, tucking the birth certificate into my pocket. I felt like I was in a daze.

Then Lou's arm was tugging at my sleeve, pulling me toward the door. Winnie looked up at us, cocked her head, and whined.

"Shhhh," Lou cooed. "Quiet, girl."

She cracked the door open and slipped out, pulling me with her.

I was halfway out when an enormous peal of thunder cracked down over us. The sound made Winnie howl and shook Mr. Bailey out of his stupor, causing his eyes to whip up and look straight at us.

I heard Lou gasp. "Run!" she yelled as she reached the bottom of the steps.

Behind us, Winnie was scratching like mad at the door. I hesitated.

"What are you doing?" Lou cried. "He's coming!"

Mr. Bailey was indeed charging toward us. I had mere seconds before he would reach me. I felt a hard knot land in my stomach like I had swallowed a cherry pit. Fear seeped through me. Everything in my body said to run.

But there was Winnie. Trapped in that dark house, just like Jack had been.

Before I knew what I was doing, I was running back up the steps. I threw the door open wide, and Winnie tumbled out.

Then we were all running. Lou first, then Winnie, then me, then Mr. Bailey. I could feel him gaining on me, hear him shouting as I made for the woods. I hadn't yet reached the old pickup when he lunged forward and grabbed my leg, sending me sprawling. My hands landed in the dirt, cushioning the blow, but not in time to stop my head from banging into the bumper of the truck. Pain shot through my face.

Mr. Bailey was pulling me backward by my leg, but then Lou had reached for my arm and was tugging me forward.

"Get off him!" she was shouting. "Get your sorry hands off or else!"

For the second time that morning, she picked up a rock and hurled it, hitting Mr. Bailey in the jaw. He gave a cry of pain, and the next instant, I was free. I scrambled up, holding one hand to my throbbing eye, and followed Lou.

"Winnie!" I called. "Come on, girl!"

But she was already there at my heels. As the skies tore open, the three of us reached the trees and kept on running, not one of us daring to look back.

34

Lou and I had to go our separate ways as soon as we reached the safety of the road. She had to get home before Mrs. Maguire found her missing. I, on the other hand, found myself pedaling toward the graveyard, where I could be on my own to think.

The storm had passed, and I sat on a bench in the dappled sunshine. Winnie darted back and forth in front of me, chasing crickets in the grass.

My face throbbed where it had hit the bumper of the truck, and I suspected I'd have a black eye. My mind felt all jumbled up, just like the Baileys' cabin had been. Clearly, Mr. Bailey hadn't done much to keep it clean since Jack's disappearance. But there were no clues to suggest any kind of violence. And if Mr. Bailey wasn't even capable of picking up a broom, I wasn't sure how he could manage to clean up a crime scene or cover up a murder.

That thought should have been a relief, and it was.

But then there was the matter of the birth certificate.

I took it out of my pocket and unfolded it. I looked again over all the details to make sure I hadn't made a mistake. My eyes fell on Jack's date of birth.

I had forgotten. Today was his birthday.

Lou had been wrong. She'd said there were three possibilities for why Jack had gone missing—either there was an accident, or he had run away, or there was foul play. But there was another possibility. One that had been right in front of me all along, but which I had refused to see.

I rose to my feet. Except instead of picking up my bike and heading for the gate, I gazed around the headstones, searching.

I'm not sure why I wanted to find Mrs. Bailey's gravestone. I think maybe I wanted to feel close to her, the only other person who had cared for Jack as much as I had. Maybe, too, I wanted to make sure she was actually there. That Jack had at least told me the truth about something.

I finally spotted her name on a small stone in a

shady corner of the graveyard. Moss was creeping up its side. Her first name had been Sarah, and she had died in 1933. I wondered if she was lonely down there by herself.

"I bet you miss him, too," I whispered to the stone as Winnie weaved around my legs.

Then something else caught my eye. A flash of color among the grass that grew in untidy clumps around the stone. I knelt down and plucked it from the ground, where it had been planted like a flag.

It was brilliant turquoise feather.

One Week Before

June 1943

"It's your birthday next week," I said.

Jack looked up from the worm he was currently using to bait his line. We had spent the golden afternoon hours diving into the freezing water and lying on the dock in the warm sun. When the storm clouds had come rolling in, I was about to say we should head home, but then Jack suggested we stay a while longer to fish.

"I guess it is," replied Jack. His voice was quiet.

"Sixteen," I mused. "I can't wait to be sixteen."

He bumped my shoulder. "Don't be trying to grow up so fast."

Which made me wish I had kept my almost-thirteen-year-old mouth shut.

"Mama says to come over and she'll fix you supper," I said. "Whatever you want. We saved up our meat coupons especially."

I tried not to betray my excitement. The truth was, Mama and I had happened across a burgundy Roadmaster the week before in the garage of a woman in Asheville who was selling Mama a used bassinet and buggy.

When Mama had asked about buying the bike, the woman had looked at it a long time before saying her boy wouldn't be needing it anymore, so we might as well have it, too.

The bike was going to be Jack's sixteenth birthday present. So he wouldn't have to ride his rusty old rattler around anymore. If he protested, Mama would say it was just an investment in the business.

But Jack wasn't to know any of that until the birthday dinner.

"That's nice of her," he said, eyes flicking toward a shadow in the water. "Your folks have always been real good to me."

"But you . . . since Daddy left, I mean—you've been good to us, too. To me."

I think it was the memory of Mrs. Musgrave that made me come out and say it. Mama had been so down ever since the Musgraves had left, and it had made me realize just how much Mrs. Musgrave's friendship had meant to Mama. I hoped she knew.

"Don't know what you mean," Jack said.

"You do," I said. "You've always looked out for me. I—I don't know what I'd do without you."

Jack didn't say anything for a long moment, and I felt my cheeks go warm. He wasn't the sort of boy who liked compliments.

"You'd do just fine, Danny," he said finally. "Hear me? You'd be just fine."

Rain began to fall around us, dimpling the river.

"Looks like a hard rain coming in," Jack said, squinting at the sky. "And nothing here wants to bite. Guess we'd better head out."

He sounded disappointed, but then why would he be in a hurry to return home to his father?

"You can come for dinner tonight, too," I said. I knew Mama wouldn't mind.

But Jack shook his head. "It might thunder. Winnie hates that. She always needs someone to hold her through a thunderstorm. Otherwise she goes nuts."

Then he turned to me. "You go on," he said. "I'll pack up here."

"I can help," I replied.

"Naw," he insisted. "Your mama will worry, and then she'll be mad at me for keeping you. You go on."

I shrugged. "All right, Jack. See you tomorrow."

His crooked-toothed smile started in the righthand

corner of his mouth, then slowly spread over his whole face. It was a warm smile. A catching smile. A things-are-gonna-be-all-right smile.

"See you around, Danny."

I hopped on my bike. When I turned back, Jack was still there, watching me go. But he wasn't smiling any longer.

35

June 1943

When I got home from the graveyard, I tiptoed up the front steps with Winnie at my heels.

With any luck, Mama would be sleeping. Then I could sneak in and figure out some story to tell her about the dog and my eye, which was still aching.

"Danny?" she called, the instant I walked in. "Is that you?"

She was standing in the kitchen with her back to me.

"You're supposed to be in bed," I said weakly.

"Goodness, who died and made you Dr. Pe—" she started. But then Winnie barreled over to her and began nipping at the bottom of her housecoat. "What on earth!"

She turned in confusion, then caught sight of me and gasped. "Danny, your eye!"

This was all going terribly wrong. Mama should have been resting, not getting all riled up because of me. What if she fainted again, or worse?

She quickly gave Winnie a bite of cheese to stop her frantic nipping, then wiped her hands against the apron that always hung on the wall. It was pink, just like Mrs. Bailey's. Mama was sweeping toward me, but I couldn't stop staring at the apron, imagining if it was all I had left of her.

I wrapped my arms around her and squeezed.

Mama hugged me back tightly, her belly solid and round between us. "What's all this about?" she asked, when I finally released her. Then her eyes widened. "Oh, Danny. You didn't go to Mr. Bailey's, did you? Did he—"

"No," I said quickly.

I wanted to tell Mama everything. About breaking into the Baileys' house. About finding the birth certificate and the feather in the graveyard. I wanted to tell her that I thought I finally knew what had happened to Jack.

But she could never find out about Mr. Bailey. At least, not until she delivered the baby safely. It might give her a heart attack to think of me breaking into his cabin.

"I—I found Winnie on my paper route," I said. "She

was wandering around down by the river. Mr. Bailey must have kicked her out."

"And your eye? No, wait, I need to get some ice on it this second."

She led me to the sofa and disappeared back into the kitchen, returning a moment later with chipped ice that had been wrapped in a clean rag. Sitting down next to me, she tenderly applied it to my eye.

"I'm fine, Mama," I said. "You need to be in bed."

"Don't take this the wrong way, sweetheart," she replied shortly, "but the last thing I need is one more person trying to tell me what to do. I'd much rather you tell me what happened."

"I fell off my bike." I didn't dare to look at her. "When I was chasing after Winnie. She was scared, Mama. I don't think Mr. Bailey has been treating her right."

The dog had curled up at my feet and was already fast asleep.

Mama looked at me a long hard minute before the dark lines between her brows faded, like birds disappearing into the clouds. "And this has nothing to do with finding Jack?"

I nearly broke down and told her everything then. Nearly pulled out the birth certificate in my pocket.

The one that had been written in 1925.

Which meant that today wasn't Jack's sixteenth birthday.

It was his *eighteenth.*

Had he ever actually told me he was going to be sixteen? Or had I simply assumed because that was the age tenth graders normally were?

It didn't matter. One way or another, Jack was eighteen now. Old enough to go to war—to enlist without a parent's permission. Jack hadn't run away from Foggy Gap. He had run *to* the war.

All along, the answer had been staring me in the face. Because if there was one thing I knew about Jack Bailey, it was that he was a hero.

He just hadn't wanted to be *my* hero anymore.

I wondered if he would have told me the truth if I hadn't opened my big mouth that last afternoon on the dock. *I don't know what I'd do without you.* Because how could he have told me after that? That he was leaving me, too, just like Daddy had. That he might not be coming back, either.

Instead, he'd carved *YONDER* into that tree and snuck away. He must have thought he was doing me a kindness. Letting me believe that he'd gone off in search of some magical town instead of to war. That way, I wouldn't have to worry about him, too.

I supposed in a way I should be grateful for Mr. Bailey. Jack probably would have enlisted the moment we had entered the war if his father had given his permission. He had, I realized, already been sixteen then. But Jack had told me that Mr. Bailey would never have agreed to let him go.

I also thought I understood now why the police had gone to see Mr. Bunch. As a member of the draft board, Mr. Bunch would know that Jack had enlisted. Sergeant Womack was there to ask him not to tell Mr. Bailey where Jack had gone. Because maybe, just maybe, Jack had been right about Mr. Bailey not being all bad. If deep down, some part of him really did care for Jack, then maybe he had wanted to keep Jack home to spare him from living through the same things he had. And Sergeant Womack wanted to protect Mr. Bailey from the truth just as Jack had wanted to protect me.

The only person Jack *had* said goodbye to was his mother. That was why I had put the turquoise feather back where it had been planted by her tombstone. It was a goodbye that wasn't meant for me.

"Danny?" Mama asked.

"Huh?" I had sunken into my thoughts, forgetting my own mother was still standing right in front of me.

"Does all this have anything to do with you trying to find Jack?"

I couldn't summon any words, so I simply shook my head. This time, the truth was my weight to bear.

36

WEDNESDAY

When I awoke the next morning, the deepest of the night's shadows still clung to the shapes around me, turning them all to phantoms. The morning before, I had felt so heavy getting out of bed. But that day, I just felt hollow.

I thought I heard rustling coming from Mama's room as I passed. I knocked on the door very softly.

"It's too early," I heard her groan.

So I went on my way. I rode slowly into town, dark and still as a theater holding its breath for the curtain to go up. The only sign of life was the smell of wood-smoke from somewhere off in the hills, and the distant sound of a rooster crowing.

I didn't see the houses as I delivered their papers, not really. My eyes lingered only over Dylan Price's home, and the gold star in the window. An entire life traded for a stitched star against a drawn shade.

Was Jack worried that he might never come home? Would he ever write to me to explain himself? Even now, I wanted the chance to tell him that I wasn't angry at him for going. That I would have understood. I just wished he had trusted me enough to tell me.

The only thing I still couldn't make sense of was the bird I had seen. I thought of it as I came to the little bridge that arched over the stream.

If not for the feather I had found at Sarah Bailey's grave, I might have thought I'd simply imagined the bird. But I had held that feather between my own fingers. So where had the bird come from?

My mind emptied as I mustered the energy to get up the steep road to the Widow Wagner's house. Slowly, it appeared over the hill. It would have looked cheerful if it weren't for the drawn curtains—heavy dark drapes in the second-story windows and delicate lace curtains below.

Even as I thought this, one of the lace curtains twitched, and I couldn't help but glance at the window. I half expected to see the Widow Wagner peering out at me, but instead it was the beady eyes of her raven.

A raven would have been a strange pet for anyone

else, but it made a certain kind of sense for a witch. So I had never questioned it before. But in that moment, I did. Because witches, like fairy-tale towns, are for stories. The frail woman Lou and I had seen on the morning her house had been vandalized was no witch. She was a lonely old lady, just like Jack had said.

Though she must not have been completely alone in the world, because someone had cleaned that graffiti off her house.

Now that I thought about it, why *did* an old woman keep a raven for a pet?

I felt a jolt in my chest, like someone had struck a match there.

What if the raven wasn't her only pet bird?

It hadn't been far from here that I had seen the jewelbird flying from tree to tree. What if it wasn't escaped from a circus, or some magical town? What if all along it lived right here, in this house? And what if Jack, too, had realized where it had come from?

I squeezed my eyes shut, trying to recall exactly what it was Jack had said about the widow.

The widow is just a harmless old lady. The kind who knits scarves and keeps butterscotches in her pockets.

It had never occurred to me that he might have been speaking from his own knowledge. But the widow *had* smelled like butterscotch the morning Lou and I had seen her. And there was the checkered scarf Jack had taken to wearing last winter, the one I had seen in his drawer the day before. I had thought it must have been donated by the church but—

I pictured the widow again, standing in front of me and Lou on Sunday morning, a blanket pulled round her shoulders. A knit blanket, checkered blue and white, just like Jack's scarf.

Had the *widow* made it for Jack?

Before I knew what I was doing, I had thrown my bike down in the grass and was running up the widow's lawn to her door. For once, I was not afraid. If the widow knew something I didn't, I had to find out.

I banged on the front door. "Hello?" I called. "Mrs. Wagner?"

I thought I heard a rustling sound from inside, but the door didn't open. I banged again.

"It's Danny Timmons," I called. "Your paperboy."

I was about to bang a third time, when suddenly the door cracked open, revealing a shadowy figure inside.

"Hello, Danny," came a quiet voice. "I guess you had better come in."

The door opened wider.

Then the shadow became a boy, and the boy became Jack Bailey. Stepping out of the darkness like a ghost pulled back from the great black beyond.

37

"You're—you're here," I sputtered.

The corner of Jack's lips twitched as though he were going to smile, but he couldn't quite bring himself to do it.

"I guess the jig is up," he said, peering out behind me before sweeping me into the dark house.

Nothing—none of the stories about the widow, not even seeing her in the forest—could have prepared me for what I saw inside.

Cages of brass, wood, silver, and copper sat on every table. They hung from the mantel and even the ceiling. You couldn't have stood up from the sofa without knocking into one. Most of them were empty, but in one that hung by the curtained window, a robin hopped back and forth, chirping. In another, a great horned owl was hunched over in sleep. And there, perched atop a chair by the fireplace, was the jewel-bird, staring calmly at me from the gloom.

I gasped, taking a step forward.

Caaaaw!

The enormous raven flapped its wings from its perch on the nearest windowsill, pointing its sharp beak in my direction like a robber might have pointed a knife. I lifted my hands to protect my face, but the crow flew right past me and out the door.

"It's all right," Jack said, shutting the door after it. "She won't hurt you. She's well-trained."

I didn't move. *What was Jack doing here?*

"You're by yourself?" he asked. He kept his voice very low.

I nodded. "Are you . . . are you hiding?"

"You could say that," he said. Then, studying my face, "What happened to your eye?"

I could hear the worry threading through his voice as he asked the question I had never asked him. My hand went instinctively to my bruise.

"It's nothing," I said.

"All right, then," Jack replied. "Let's sit." He nudged my shoulder with his own, and I felt a little shudder of surprise at his touch. Like it wasn't until then that

I believed the flesh and bones of him. That he wasn't some kind of trick or mirage.

I followed into the sitting room, where he ducked beneath the hanging birdcages to sit on a green, wood-backed sofa, embroidered with pink flowers. It creaked beneath his weight, clearly meant for a more delicate creature. I sat warily beside him, glancing over at the jewelbird, which hadn't moved a muscle since I had entered.

"How did you figure it out?" Jack asked. Now that my eyes had adjusted, I saw his narrow face looked sallow, like he hadn't seen sunlight for days. I wished we could open a curtain.

"I didn't," I said. "I only came because I saw that bird nearby, and I realized that you must have been coming here to visit the widow. Your scarf. She made it for you. And you knew she liked butterscotch. But I didn't realize you were here. I—I thought you'd gone off to war. I found your birth certificate."

"Oh," Jack breathed. It felt like something slipped away on his breath, like a letting go.

"So? Are you going to tell me what's going on?" My voice was sharp like the raven's beak. I, too, was beginning to feel something slipping from me, and I needed Jack to put it back in place.

"The widow loves birds," Jack said, gesturing to the bird on the chair. Even in the darkness, its brilliant

{262}

feathers shone. "She finds wounded ones in the forest and brings them here. She nurses them back to health if she can. Gives them a home if she can't. She's tried to release this one, but he keeps coming back. Carolina parakeets are loyal birds."

As if on cue, the bird fluttered its wings and flew across the room, landing without a sound on Jack's shoulder. He reached up and stroked its back.

"Parakeet?" I asked, staring in awe. "I thought it was a—a jewelbird."

"Two names for the same thing, maybe. I didn't believe the widow when she told me that's what he was, not 'til she showed me a picture in a book. Those birds are supposed to be extinct. People shot them for their feathers, to put in hats and things. And when one would get shot, the others wouldn't fly away like they should have done. They flocked around the bleeding one, trying to help it. It made them easy targets. But I guess there were some left somewhere out there."

He was talking too fast, rambling in a way he'd never done before. But I heard the way the words stuck in his dry mouth.

"I know you're scared of her," he went on, "but she's a nice lady. Honest. When I followed the bird here the first time, she invited me in, gave me some soup. She recognized me from delivering her paper. She told me to come back for breakfast, and then the next day, too.

I think she liked the company."

"I still don't understand," I said. Frustration bubbled up from somewhere dark, like cold water from an underground spring. Jack was dancing around something, with all his talk of breakfasts and birds, and I was sick of spinning with him. "Why are you here, Jack? I thought you might have been killed. First, I thought your father might've done it. I nearly said as much to the police! And then I thought you'd drowned. And then that you had gone off to find Yonder. Then I realized you had gone to war. But here you are."

"I didn't mean you to think I had drowned," Jack replied. "Only everyone else. I figured, see, that you'd tell the police about my bike—that it was right where I'd left it the last time you saw me. They'd know about the storm and put two and two together. But I left you the message, carved into the tree. *Yonder.* I knew you'd understand it but no one else would. Even if you tried to tell them, who would believe you, except maybe your mama? Everyone else would think I had drowned, but you and your family would know I was all right. That's how I meant it."

The air seemed to grow heavier. The dark was pressing down around me. "You mean you . . . you wanted people to think you were dead?"

He dropped his head into his hands and pulled at his brown unkempt hair. When he looked up again,

{264}

even in the blue-black darkness of the house, I could see there were tears shining on his cheeks. And I knew then that he was in a bad way, because I had never seen Jack Bailey really cry. Not when he had shown up at the *Herald* office, bruised and bloody. Not when his father turned up to take him home again. Not even when he spoke about his mother.

"But why'd you do it?" I asked. Trying not to think of how badly I'd wanted to find Jack, and how all along, he hadn't wanted to be found.

His eyes searched the room, like in one of those birdcages he might find the courage to say what needed to be said.

"You said you found my birth certificate?" he asked finally.

I nodded. "I thought you were turning sixteen."

"You know I've never been much good at school," Jack said, the sheepish ghost of a smile flitting across his face. "When Mama died, I lost the taste for it. And my father liked it better when I stayed home anyway. I missed six months before Mr. Rowlands told him I was a truant and started hauling me in every other day. I had to do third grade all over again. And I never quite caught up. I got held back again two years later."

Then he pulled a piece of paper from his pocket and handed it over to me.

"I can't do it, Danny," Jack said. "I can't go to war."

I understood then that Jack wasn't dancing in circles anymore. All along, he had been leading me, ever so gently, down the winding path to truth. And finally, we had reached its end.

38

The letter in my hand had been sent from the draft board. It informed Jack that he was being drafted and gave him a time to appear for a health inspection by Dr. Penny. It was signed by Nick Pittman.

So Jack hadn't enlisted. He was going to be drafted. Mr. Pittman had found a way to run him out of town after all, just like he'd run out the Musgraves.

"You're—you're saying you're a draft dodger?" I asked.

I stared at him, saw how he flinched at the last two words. It was like I was looking at a stranger.

How could this boy—or was he a man now?—be the same one who had saved the Coombs twins from the flood? Who had saved *me* from Bruce?

I knew Jack Bailey was brave like the water was wet and the sky was blue. *Everyone* knew it. Yet my certainty was being swept away, and I wondered if that was how the Coombs twins had felt when the floodwater had lifted them off their feet in their own front doorway.

"I'm not afraid of war," Jack said, and for the first time there was a guarded clip to his words. "I'm not a coward. At least, not in the way you're probably thinking."

"Then why?" I asked, desperate for an answer I could make sense of.

"Because of *him*," Jack replied bitterly. "Because of my father. He never really came back from the war. Or if he did, he brought it back with him. Inside of him. And he'll never be done fighting it. You've seen what kind of man he is, Danny."

My mind skipped from memory to memory, a stone over troubled waters.

Mr. Bailey's mean eyes, his spitting words. *You all think he's so* good. *If my son's so good, then where is he?*

Jack's voice cutting across the sound of the river. *He was the gentlest man my mother had ever met.*

The war medal underneath Jack's bed, buried in the dark like a cursed pirate treasure.

Jack looked at me, something I'd never seen flitting across his face. For a moment, it felt almost like an accusation. The bird on his shoulder was staring at me with its black eyes. My toes scrunched up in my shoes.

"I've as good as given up my whole life so far to him," Jack said. "No matter how bad things got, I stayed. I was loyal. Even now, I don't *want* to leave. This is my home. It's all I know. But I can't—I won't become him. Can you understand that?"

"You're not him, Jack," I replied, almost pleading. "You could never be him."

"But I feel it sometimes. It's there inside me, I know it. That rage. It's like a mean old dog. Sleeping most of the time, but every once in a while, it gets taken by surprise and wakes up. I can keep it locked inside of me now. But I just know that if they send me to war, I won't be able to keep it in anymore. And it won't be me who comes back. It'll be that rage. It'll be my father."

"Don't say that," I murmured. "Of course it would be you."

Even as I said it, I thought of the way Jack had drawn back his fist at Bruce that day I had first met him. Afterward, I thought Jack had only meant to scare him. But in the moment, I hadn't been so sure. And whatever Bruce had seen in Jack *had* scared him, bad enough for him to leave me alone after that. For a while, anyway.

"I won't do what he's done to me to some other

boy," Jack said. "To *anyone*."

Maybe Jack was enough of a man in the eyes of the law to be drafted, but in that moment, he seemed so small. Not that much taller than me, since I'd had my growth spurt last winter. His cheeks were still smooth, and his voice was as gentle as the first breath of spring.

"You went back," I said numbly. "We wanted you to stay, but you went back."

That's why I had told myself that whatever happened in that little cabin couldn't be so bad. That Jack was strong enough to bear it alone. And so I had never once asked him about it again after that first time. I hadn't wanted to know.

He had only been a boy, just like me.

"Well, I can't go back again," he said. "I have to go."

"But not like this!" I cried. "Not by playing dead and sneaking away! Not b-by turning your back on everyone. Please don't go, Jack!"

My voice broke as I said his name, and the tears I had been holding back for days finally began to fall. I felt a hand on my shoulder, warm and sturdy.

"It's okay, Danny," Jack murmured. "It's all right."

As I began to cry, I felt the relief of a fever breaking. The moment before the raw, bracing cold that washes in after. I knew as long as I stayed there, with Jack's hand on my shoulder, things would be all right. He could stay Jack Bailey, my hero.

And I knew, too, that when he pulled away, everything would be different forever. Because his hand on my shoulder felt like goodbye. Just like Daddy's embrace had before he boarded the bus that would take him to war.

"What did Daddy say to you?" I asked when I could finally speak again. "Just before he got on the bus? He whispered something in your ear."

Jack hesitated.

"He told me to remember I only had one life," said Jack. "He told me to make it count."

"Oh," I breathed. That sounded like the kind of good advice Daddy would give. And yet, I wondered if it was those words that had made Jack start thinking about leaving. One goodbye beginning another.

I tried to find a dignified way to wipe my wrist under my nose. "I still don't understand. Why are you here? If you wanted to run away, why didn't you?"

"The widow. She's sick. She doesn't have anybody. Her husband is dead, and she doesn't know where the rest of her family is anymore. She hasn't heard from them since they left Germany a few years ago. So I told her I would stay until the end. She doesn't have long. Then I'll be gone. She's given me some things to take."

I felt a warm jealousy that stung like the thimbleful of brandy Mama gave me when I had a sore throat.

Jack had trusted the Widow Wagner with his secret, but he hadn't trusted me.

"Why didn't you tell me?"

"I guess I didn't want you to think of me the way you probably do now," he said. "I know how people talk about George Maguire. I didn't want you to remember me that way. Too late for that now, huh?"

I could feel it *was* too late even as I tried to convince myself it wasn't. I would never see Jack the same way again.

But I still wanted him to stay. And I couldn't make sense of why he needed to disappear so badly. There were all sorts of reasons a man could get out of being drafted without skulking off like a thief in the night.

"But if you just explain to the draft board," I said, "You're still in high school! They'll let you graduate before they send you anywhere."

"I flunked out," Jack said, shaking his head. "I've been flunking math all year. Mr. Bunch made me a deal that if I could pass the final exam, he would pass me, but I knew I'd never be able to do it."

So *that* was the deal Mr. Bunch had mentioned.

"But I could have helped you!" I protested. The jewelbird gave an anxious flutter at my raised voice.

"Only if you took the test for me," he said. "It was hopeless, Danny."

"Then . . . then . . . you could get work as a farmhand!

Farm labor is exempt from the draft, isn't it?"

Jack sighed. "That's what I thought I'd do at first, too. But most of the farms around here are owned by Mr. Pittman. Who also happens to be on the draft board. You remember that day we overheard your mama talking to Mrs. Musgrave?"

I nodded.

"I realized that day Mr. Pittman was never going to give up a chance to send me to war. Mrs. Musgrave was right. Once he's made up his mind he wants something, nobody around here is going to get him to change it. And he wanted me gone. That's when I knew I was going to have to disappear.

"It's better like this anyway, Danny," Jack said gently. "Better that I get a new start. I'm going to do my bit for the war, I swear. I saw a place in Tennessee advertising for coal miners in the paper. Roosevelt is always going on about how important miners are, isn't he?"

"What about Winnie?" I asked weakly. Playing the last card in my losing hand.

A look of longing crossed Jack's face. "You got her, right?"

"How'd you know?"

He nodded, relief washing over his face. "I told you she needs someone to hold her through a storm," he said. "I figured you'd take the hint."

"So you won't take her?"

"She needs a home. Breakfast and dinner every day. She'll be better with you."

I wasn't about to argue. At least with Winnie by my side, I would have a bit of Jack left to me.

"Jack?" called a far-off, threadbare voice. At first I thought it might have belonged to one of the birds— some kind of parrot.

Then a door cracked open on the far side of the room, and there stood the Widow Wagner. If it was possible, she looked even worse than the last time I had seen her. Her face was full of dark hollows, and she was bent over as though it hurt to stand. The jewelbird flew from Jack's shoulder to hers.

"Voices," she rasped. "I heard—"

"It's all right," Jack said, quickly standing. "He's a friend."

"Won't—tell?"

She looked from Jack to me, her eyes imploring.

"No," said Jack. "He won't tell anyone I'm here. Will you, Danny?"

For a long moment, I didn't say anything. Then, finally, I nodded.

"A good . . . boy," the widow croaked. I wasn't sure if she meant me or Jack. The corners of her lips just barely lifted, as though she were trying to smile. For an instant, I felt I finally saw beyond her aged face to the person who lived underneath. Then she and the bird disappeared behind the door.

"I should go," Jack said again, not meeting my eye. "She needs me."

I need you, too, I wanted to say. But I was too filled with shame at the stories I had repeated about the widow, the way Lou and I had run from her in the forest. Now she was the one who was coming to Jack's defense. Protecting him when I had not.

"I'll come back," I said. "Tomorrow. I'll bring you some things. Food and some money, if I can find it."

"No, Danny," he protested. "I told you, Mrs. Wagner is giving me what I need. You don't have to—"

"I'll be back tomorrow," I said firmly. I wasn't ready to say goodbye.

The floorboards creaked beneath my feet as I walked slowly to the door. Half of me didn't want to leave Jack here, in another dark, lonely house. The other half wanted nothing more than to feel the fresh sunlight on my face.

I reached out my hand for the doorknob, then paused. "After I saw the tree carving, and then I saw the bird . . . I really did wonder if maybe it was real. If maybe you had gone to try to find Yonder."

Jack's eyes softened and he smiled. A smile as good as sunlight.

"Maybe I will," he said. "Maybe one day I'll see you there, Danny."

39

As I followed the road back to where I'd abandoned my bike, my mind felt too full and my chest too heavy. In that moment, I knew what it was to be a storm cloud just before thunder roars through the sky and rain begins to pour.

I always understood that Jack and I were an unlikely pair, but I thought we had stuck together because he had seen something in me. Maybe even the same kind of courage he had in him, just buried way down deep where no one else could see. I thought if anyone could bring it out in me, it would be him.

It had never occurred to me that it was *fear* that we shared, that had brought us together.

And now it would tear us apart.

I was so wrapped up in my thoughts that when the ice truck came barreling around a corner, the driver blared his horn and I only just skidded out of the way in time.

Heart hammering, I returned to the road. But where would I go? I couldn't go home. What excuse would I give Mama this time? I would have to go to school. I would ride most of the way, I decided, then walk the last bit in case anyone was watching from a window. I would tell Mrs. Pattershaw I had gotten a flat tire.

As I rode through town, it felt like I was passing through a darkness that had been there all along but I had never noticed before. It was like all my life I had lived in Foggy Gap without ever looking up to the mountains that loomed above, casting their shadows down like nets.

Was that how Jack had felt every day of his life? Like he was walking in shadows that no one else could see?

Because all of us had decided we didn't want to.

Jack was turning his back on us, but we had all turned our backs first: Sergeant Womack, who was too loyal to Mr. Bailey to see the man his friend had become; Dr. Penny, who had seen Jack's injuries and then looked away; even Mama and Daddy, who had let him go back.

And me. Who had never brought the subject up again. Pretended not to see the bruises that came after because I didn't want to be shaken awake from the pretty dream I'd been living, in which Jack would make me strong and brave like him.

By the time the brick bell tower of the school craned its neck over the next hill, I felt queasy. When I got down to walk the rest of the way, my hands had left a slick film of sweat on my handlebars. How, I wondered, would I be able to sit in Mrs. Pattershaw's classroom all day?

As if in answer to my question, I heard someone calling my name. Lou was on the road behind me, biking like the devil was hot on her heels.

"Danny!" she called again. "Wait up!"

Another moment and she was close enough that I could see the tangles in her shorn hair and the pink in her cheeks.

"I have to go to school," I said flatly.

"No, Danny," she replied, panting with the effort of the words. "You can't. You have to go home."

My mind filled with the image of a solemn black car driving up and stopping in front of our house. Two somber-faced men getting out and walking dutifully up our front steps.

"Is it . . . is it Daddy?" I mustered the courage to ask.

"What? No, no, it's your mother."

"Mama? What's wrong with Mama?"

Lou wrinkled her nose. *"Boys,"* she muttered. And then: "She's having the baby, you nincompoop!"

For another moment, I stood where I was, firmly planted to the ground as if I had sprouted there from an acorn.

"Let's go!" Lou cried.

And we did.

40

That baby was just about the only thing that could have taken my mind off Jack.

I didn't get to go in right away. Mrs. Maguire told me and Lou we had to wait outside until everything was done.

Lou, it turned out, had come looking for me just after I had left for my route that morning. Instead of finding me, she found Mama in the middle of one of her pains, trying to get to the door so she could find a neighbor to go get Dr. Penny.

When I had knocked on Mama's door that morning and she had said it was too early, she hadn't been talking to me at all. She'd been talking to the baby, who was already on its way.

Lou had been the one to go for the doctor, and then her mother, too.

"And then I went out to find you," she explained while we waited. "I looked everywhere! Where were you?"

Fortunately, that was the moment Mrs. Maguire opened the front door and waved us in.

Mama was lying in bed, her skin pale and her hair matted with sweat. There was a sharp, metallic smell in the room. But happiness glowed out from inside her, like a lantern burning through a thick fog. And there in her arms was a tiny baby.

"Danny," Mama said, beaming with pride. "Come meet your sister."

Cautiously, I inched over to the bed. It was just me, Mama, and the baby in the room. I'd left Lou downstairs with Dr. Penny, who raised his brows at my black eye but congratulated me as he packed up his things. Like I was the one who had done something to be proud of.

When Mama nudged the baby into my trembling arms, though, I understood why he'd said it.

Happy was the last thing I'd expected to feel that day, and it *wasn't* happiness that shot through me as I looked down into my little sister's face. Not exactly.

It was more like the surprise you feel when you wake up to discover that it's snowed overnight. The shock at how quickly the world can transform into something so pure and bright.

That was how it felt looking at my baby sister, her ruddy face pinched in sleep. Every inch as ordinary as a piglet and every ounce as marvelous as an angel.

"She's perfect," I murmured, worried my voice might wake her. "And so . . . small."

"You were that size once," said Mama. "Sometimes I still think of you that way. I always will, probably."

As if part of me would always be as innocent as the baby I held in my arms.

"I'm sorry I wasn't here," I said. "I should have been here."

"Nonsense," Mama replied.

Just then, the baby shifted in my arms. Without opening her eyes, she screwed up her face and yowled like a bobcat cub. Her hands jerked out from the blanket and balled themselves into fists.

I held her out to Mama, alarmed. "What did I do wrong?"

"Nothing," Mama said, taking the baby and holding her close to her chest. "That's just what babies do. She's waking up to the world is all. It's a confusing place for her."

And on that, my sister and I were agreed.

In another moment, she had fallen asleep again against Mama, who was herself beginning to close her eyes.

I may not have known much about childbirth, but I knew this: Mama had earned a good rest. I had the strongest urge to pull back her covers and go to sleep there, too, like I had when I was small and had night-mares.

But I wasn't the baby from Mama's memory any-more. I wasn't even the boy I had been mere days ago. And though I wasn't a man yet, I felt I was something in between now.

"Can I . . . can I do anything?" I asked.

Mama wagged her head. "I've got everything I need right here," she said, sending me a drowsy smile. "Mrs. Maguire went into town for some things, but she'll be back after to help us. Such a kind woman. She doesn't deserve how she's been treated . . ."

My gut twisted like a snake coiling up to strike, but before Mama could say anything more, she had fallen asleep.

41

When Mrs. Maguire returned from the store, she sent
Lou home to take care of her younger brothers, over
Lou's complaints.

"Who on earth is going to cook supper if you don't
go?" Mrs. Maguire snapped. "Your father?"

She gave a dry snort at this thought, as though she
might as well ask him to grow wings and fly. Finally,
Lou relented, but not before she took a peek at the
baby and declared her the spitting image of Winston
Churchill. Thankfully, Mama was still asleep.

I didn't want her to go, either. I dreaded being alone
with Mrs. Maguire. Those eyes, sharpened by the
years of raising three mischievous boys (not to mention Lou), seemed like they could cut right through

a person. Strip away a lie as easy as an apple peel to find the truth underneath.

And my truth—the truth about me and Lou—was rotten.

I shouldn't have been worried, though. Mrs. Maguire didn't have a glance to spare for me, only occasional orders to bark in my direction. She set me to work chopping vegetables for our stew while she went out back to do the wash. And no sooner had she served up dinner than the baby was howling once more, and she left me alone at the table to eat.

"Do you know how to wash dishes?" she asked as she wiped her hands on Mama's apron, which she'd strung around her own waist.

"Yes, ma'am," I said.

"Good," she replied. "Maybe I'll send Lou for lessons."

And that was the most she said until later that night, when she reappeared at the bottom of the stairs.

"Good night, then," she said. "I'll look in tomorrow morning. You come for me if you need anything in the night, hear?"

I nodded, but Mrs. Maguire was already walking briskly to the door.

"We won't, will we?" I asked suddenly. "Need anything? I mean, Mama and the baby—they're both all right?"

Mrs. Maguire hesitated and softened, like someone

who's just stepped into the warm sun. "They're fine," she said. "They make a fine pair, and you'll make a fine brother. Nothing makes you want to be better like a new baby. It's a fresh start, hmm?"

She looked hard at me then, and I wondered if she had seen right through me after all.

42

As I tiptoed down the hall to my room that night, ready to drop straight into bed, I heard a sound coming from Mama's room. A rustling and a kind of mewling. The door was cracked open, so I peeked in.

The room was awash with moonlight. The baby was stirring in her bassinet, which Mrs. Maguire must have moved into Mama's room. Mama was deep asleep.

I hesitated for a moment, then went in and scooped the baby up. She was just a little head poking out of a knotted blanket. As I lifted her from the bassinet, she made a grunting noise, but her eyes were still closed.

Carefully, I carried her over to the chair by the

window and cradled her in my lap. Outside, the stars were bright and near, as though they had crept down from their perches to get a better look at her.

Even in the quiet dark, the house felt more alive with her in it. The air trembled like the second just before a fiddle begins its song. It felt like it had when Jack had come to stay.

Funny, how I'd thought then that I had gained a big brother. And now I had a little sister.

She was so light in my arms, swaddled in her blanket like a baby bird in a nest. And me the sturdy tree holding her, keeping her safe.

I thought of what Mrs. Maguire had said, about a baby making you want to be better. My sister made me want to be braver. The kind of brother who would protect her from anything.

But even as I vowed that I would do everything I could to keep her safe in the world, I knew there were things I could not protect her from. Things like war, or stubbed toes, or thunderstorms. Like plain bad luck.

It occurred to me then that all around the world, there were probably babies that had just been born, and my little sister could have been any of them. She could have been born to movie stars in Hollywood or cowboys in Wyoming. Or she could have been born to a man like Mr. Bailey. Instead of sleeping under the clear sky, she could right now be sleeping under the bombs falling in Italy. Or worse, in a Polish ghetto. A German camp.

And what about those babies? Didn't they deserve someone to protect them, too?

It made my stomach clench to think about it. About how we all talked about what a just and necessary war we were fighting, but there were so many injustices we never spoke about at all. That we did our best to ignore.

Daddy hadn't ignored what he'd heard about the camps. He had gone off to fight. He was doing his part.

And Mama had published those articles in the paper, even though Mr. Maynard had threatened to fire her. Just so people might see what was happening.

So what was I going to do? How could I make a difference to anybody?

Though I was bone-tired, I sat up a long time looking at the baby in my arms and thinking about that question. But the answer didn't come.

It wouldn't come until the next morning, when the package from the Musgraves arrived.

43

THURSDAY

The box was on our table by the door that morning.

"Mrs. Maguire must have brought it back from Dinwiddie's yesterday," Mama said. "It'll have crossed paths with the one I sent last week, I bet."

She was sitting up in bed, looking chipper as a robin despite the racoon circles around her eyes. I probably had them, too. The baby's cries had woken me up twice in the short night. Now that Mama and I were up, my sister slept.

Mama took a bite of the toast with blackberry jam I'd brought her and gestured for me to open the box. Inside was a tiny white nightdress with a lacy collar. "Well, isn't that beautiful," Mama said, brushing the dress with her clean hand. "Is there a note?"

I pulled out the little envelope that sat at the bottom of the box and passed it to Mama, but she shook her head. "You read while I eat," she said. "The baby will be up any minute."

So I unfolded the paper inside and began to read Mrs. Musgrave's words.

Dear Pearl,

Thank you for your letter, which I received last week. I hope this package will arrive before your time does, and you'll be able to use this with the new baby. I have prayed that it will be healthy, hearty, and a good sleeper (this last prayer is for you).

You asked in your letter how we are getting on, and the answer is better than most. While I miss my home in the hills like I might a missing limb, it is wonderful to be around family again. My sister and I stay up long past all the others every night, sitting out on her stoop and making up for lost time. We have to keep our voices down unless we want the neighbors to hear. Sometimes I feel like in this city there isn't room to scratch your nose without knocking into someone else. And yet, folks take care of each other here. There are so many like us, who have come north in search of something better.

Jordan has taken to life here like a fish to water. He spends most of his time exploring the neighborhood with his cousins and is counting the days until he starts school in the fall. I will be starting with him, as I have just accepted an offer to teach the fourth grade. I am singing again, too, in the choir. I had forgotten the sweetness of hearing my voice in harmony with so many others.

It is not the life we meant to build, but if it is the one we are to lead, we will fill it with hope and love and joy.

We must also build it, for now at least, without my Anthony, who has been accepted into the army, and will have shipped out by the time you get this. Truthfully, I think he would have gone long ago if not for the farm, and for the fact that he would most likely have been denied on account of his race. I think he hopes to be the next Doris Miller. He says fighting abroad is the path to equality here. Everywhere he goes, he wears a badge with the double V on it. Victory for the Allies overseas and victory for true democracy at home. I suppose he will fight for the country he loves so that his *countrymen might love him, too.*

He's not even gone yet, and I lie awake at
night and wonder if he will come home safe.
I'm sure you feel the same for your Alan. But I
am proud, too. So very proud.

Please write and let me know how you get
on with the baby. I wish you all the luck in the
world.

Yours,
Daphne Musgrave

"Mama?"

I had finished reading the letter, but she was still
looking out the window, lost in her own thoughts.

"Well," she said finally, "I'm glad things have turned
out all right for them."

"Me too," I said. The idea of Jordan in school made
me smile.

"Who's Doris Miller?" I asked.

"A cook in the navy. Or he was a cook. That's all
they would let him be because of his race. Until Pearl
Harbor. Then he became a hero."

"So that's why Mr. Musgrave wanted to enlist?" I
asked. "To become a hero?"

"I think it's like Mrs. Musgrave says," Mama replied.
"I think he's fighting to help win the war, but also to
be seen for more than the color of his skin. I imagine

he's not the only one. I imagine some of those men will die just trying to be seen. I only hope he's right, and that he'll return home to a changed country."

"*You* see the Musgraves," I said. "Why can you see them for who they are when other people don't?"

Mama gazed at the baby. "I think most of us have a voice," she said, "somewhere deep inside us, that tells us when we've done wrong. Some people can ignore it. In fact, I'd say most of us do from time to time. But for me, there came a day when I couldn't ignore that voice anymore. I listened."

"What day?"

She lifted her hand to her collarbone, running her hands over the pale skin there. "Growing up, there was a little girl," she said, "the same age as me. We would pass each other every morning on our way to our schools, which were segregated of course. I'm not sure either of us took much notice of the other. Then one Easter, my mother got me a chain with a little golden cross that I had seen in a shop window. It was the most beautiful thing I had ever laid eyes on."

"The one you wear on Sundays?" I asked.

"That's right," said Mama. "The next week, I set off for school with the cross around my neck. Like usual, I passed the girl, and I saw her looking at my necklace. And then she smiled at me and pulled out a necklace of her own from under the collar of her dress. It was almost identical to mine. She told me it had been her mother's. From then on, we always said hello, or waved at one another if we were on opposite sides of the street. All it took was that cross to show me that as much as the world wanted us to think we were different, our hearts had so much in common. I couldn't unsee it then, how the thing that really separated us wasn't the color of our skin but how we were treated for it."

I let my eyes rest on the baby, who was twitching in her sleep, and thought again of how she could have been born anybody at all, and how the world might have treated her so different just because of where she'd been born or what she looked like. I understood what Mama meant about suddenly seeing something that had been there all the time.

"The world isn't a very fair place, is it, Mama?"

Mama cast a sad smile in my direction. She reached forward and smoothed back my hair. "No, Danny, it's not. I wish you didn't have to know that yet, but I sometimes think I should have taught you to understand more earlier. Because we can't make things right until we can see what's wrong. And we must all do our part."

"But what's *my* part?"

I didn't edit a newspaper like Mama. I was too young to fight in the war. Too late to save Jack from his father or to help the Musgraves stay in Foggy Gap.

Mama looked at me for a long minute. "I can't tell you that, Danny," she said. "Only your heart can. But if I've done my job, I'll bet you already know."

She was right. Because there *was* a voice in the back of my head, like someone calling to me from across a canyon, just like the one Mama had described. Telling me that I knew where I had to start.

There was one wrong I needed to fix more than any other. And as it turned out, I would get my chance that very day.

44

When I left the house for my paper route that morning, I took Winnie with me. I still held out the faint hope that if I couldn't convince Jack to stay, *she* could.

The houses rushed by in a blur as I raced toward the *Herald* office. We had set out a bit later than I usually did, and I was eager to get to the Widow Wagner's house to see Jack.

I had put Winnie on the leash, since we were going into town, and tied the leash to my handlebar. Her tongue lolled as she raced beside me into the wind, so happy and carefree I nearly wished we could trade places.

Once I had picked up the papers, I made my way

down Poplar Street, then swerved along my usual route. My legs flew.

As I passed by the road that shot up toward the Maguires' house, though, something moving among the trees caught my eye, and I slowed. Two boys, their backs to me, each carrying something by a handle.

It was Bruce and Logan. Even though I was late for my route, it was still plenty early. Too early to be skulking around in the woods. I came to a stop and watched closely as they moved through the trees. I saw them each give a furtive glance to one side, like they were worried about being seen.

They were headed straight for the Maguires'.

A heavy weight fell into my stomach as I squinted to make out what it was they were carrying: two buckets of paint.

I knew then exactly what was going to happen, just like I was seeing it in a movie. I knew what Bruce and Logan would do, and I knew how much it would hurt the Maguires.

I also knew that it was all because of me.

Before

November 1942

The Maguires hadn't come to church that morning. Sunday school had been lonely without Lou to interrupt Mrs. Macklenburg's lecture on the seven deadly sins with questions on how many cookies, exactly, qualified as gluttony and why, exactly, had she skipped over lust?

Of course, I understood why they hadn't come. Lou had told me the news about George as soon as she'd heard. No solemn black car for the Maguires, only a terse telegraph from the army. Mrs. Maguire had sent a note to school to say that they had all come down with a flu and hadn't left the house since.

The only blessing was that no one else knew about George's desertion.

Mama had wanted a word with Pastor Douglass after the service, so I had slipped around back to the graveyard to wait.

Once I was out of sight, I took my time, enjoying the way the autumn leaves crunched beneath my feet. The sun lit up the crimson trees from behind like a magician's trick, making them look as though they were on fire. It was warm for November, barely cool enough to need a sweater. The idea of lying back in the grass and closing my eyes was too tempting to resist.

But no sooner had my eyelids fluttered shut than I heard the sound of footsteps crunching my way. I sat up and peered around the tombstone. Bruce Pittman stood on the other side. He grinned.

"Hanging around with dead people now, huh?" he asked, as I shot up to my feet. "Well, I guess even that's better than the people you're usually with. You know, my dad says we have chickens with more brains than Jack Bailey."

"Shut up," I muttered.

I darted around the tombstone that separated us, trying to make it past him, but he shot out his foot just in time and sent me sprawling into the grass. I felt a sharp pain in my elbow and knew it must have landed on a rock.

"Oops," Bruce said.

From the ground, I searched the graveyard for anyone

else, but it was just the two of us. At school, Jack was always nearby. For a while, that had been enough to keep Bruce at bay. But we weren't at school. There was no one to help me now. I tried to scramble to my feet, but Bruce pushed me back down.

"Let me go or I'll—I'll—"

"Cry about it?" he asked. "Yell for Mommy? Rat on me?" The sun was behind him, making his expression hard to read. "Go ahead. I'll just say you're lying. Besides, only a coward would tell. Every other boy I know would fight back. But then, I guess that's what happens when your only other friend is a girl. If you can even call Lou Maguire that. Or is she your girlfriend?"

He spat the last word in disgust.

"She's not my girlfriend," I protested. "Let me go, Bruce!"

He smiled then. "Why should I?"

My heart pounded against my chest, like it had plans to run away with or without me.

I knew that I would have to give him a reason, or I would come away with worse than a bloody elbow. Bruce knew how to hurt me without leaving a mark.

"I'm not friends with Lou," I blurted out. "Why would I be friends with someone whose brother is a deserter?"

Bruce dropped his fists. His jaw went slack with disbelief. "A deserter?"

"She . . . she told me herself," I said. "I haven't spoken to her since."

Bruce's eyes glittered with glee. "Well, well," he mumbled to himself. "A deserter."

And just like that, I had taken the target off my back and set it squarely on Lou's.

I tried again to get to my feet, and this time Bruce didn't stop me. "What—what are you going to do?"

I could already see his mind calculating the possibilities. "None of your business," he said. "Since you told me the truth, I'll let you go. But I'd better not catch you speaking to that coward's sister again."

I didn't move, though. I was looking for a way to turn back time, to unsay what I had said. To undo the terrible thing I had just done to Lou and her entire family.

"Go on," Bruce commanded, like he was speaking to a dog. "Get!"

So I ran, and I didn't look back.

I did tell you, didn't I, that not all stories have a hero?

45

June 1943

I had followed Bruce's advice after that day in the graveyard. I stopped speaking to Lou. I avoided her in school, and when she came to call at the house, I ran out back where Mama couldn't find me.

I found that running away was a thing I was good at.

The news got out quickly after I told Bruce, as I had known it must. Mr. Maynard made Daddy put an article in the paper about it—the one Jack had seen. And that was about the time that the Maguires stopped showing their faces around town.

"Too ashamed," I had heard Mrs. Dinwiddie say one afternoon, when I'd gone in to fetch Mama some salt.

"As they should be," said the man she was serving at the counter. "That boy's brought shame on us all."

I wanted to tell him that he had the wrong boy.

Instead, I turned and left, and told Mama that the store had sold out.

I never told anyone what I had done. I didn't know if Lou had figured out that it had been me who'd told, or if she'd thought I was simply like everyone else . . . too appalled to associate with the Maguire family.

Now, instead of following Bruce's advice, I followed him with my eyes as he and Logan disappeared into the hemlock trees. I was filled with a sudden anger. *Enough*, said a voice in my head. *This has gone on long enough.* It was time to stop running, to stop hiding. It was time to face what I had done.

I was gathering the courage to charge after them—to stop them right then and there. But another plan suddenly appeared in my mind. A much better one. And I would have time. I was sure Bruce and Logan wouldn't be back until after nightfall. But I was going to need Lou's help.

I badly wanted to get to the widow's house—to Jack. I needed to see him, at least one more time. Maybe I would tell him what I had done. If he could still look me in the eye, then I might be able to face myself, too.

But there was somewhere else I needed to go—someone else I needed to see—even more.

Jack had been my hero. He had been, for a time, the brother I'd always wanted. But he had never been my best friend.

A best friend is someone you trust with all your secrets, who you can be your true self around. Someone who sticks to you like a burr, even when you try to pull away.

I'm not sure Jack ever had a best friend like that, but I did. Her name was Lou Maguire. She had always been a loyal friend, even when I hadn't wanted one.

She didn't deserve what I had done to her. I had to make it right. And fast.

46

Lou opened her door just a second after I knocked, like she had been waiting. She held a half-eaten apple in one hand.

"Jimmy, watch the baby!" she yelled over her shoulder. Then she stepped onto the porch and let the screen door slam shut behind her. Winnie licked her hand, and she bent down to scratch the dog behind her ears.

"Is it about the case?" she asked eagerly, sitting down on the wooden step. "Because I think we should—"

"It's not about the case," I interrupted.

She frowned. "Then what is it?"

I closed my eyes, gathering my courage. "It's about George."

Lou stiffened. "George?"

"It was me, Lou," I said. "It was me who told Bruce. I—Bruce— He was going to— But it's no excuse. I should never have done it. He must have told Mr. Pittman, who told everyone else. And I'm sorry. I'm so sorry."

They were the hardest words I had ever said, and I'd delivered them to my shoelaces, but now I glanced up. Lou wasn't looking at me, though. She was staring out at the road, frozen in place. Finally, she moved her hand slowly to her mouth and took another bite of her apple, her teeth sinking into its flesh with a loud *snap*.

Then she turned to me. "You think I didn't know?"

"You *did*?"

Lou rolled her eyes. "It wasn't a hard case to crack," she said. "Seeing as Ma and Daddy wouldn't have told anyone on their lives, and Jimmy didn't know, and it's not like the baby is going to be tattling to anyone. You were the only other person who knew. But still . . . I guess a little part of me hoped I was wrong."

"I—"

"You know Mrs. Dinwiddie doesn't speak to Ma when she goes to the market anymore? She just writes up her order without saying a word. The only person who talks to Ma less is Daddy, who can't seem to string together a single sentence anymore. And Jimmy has started wetting the bed again. Even the kids in his class know about George, and they play tricks on him now."

I fought the urge to bury my face in my hands.

"Pastor Douglass came to see us last Sunday. Ma used the rest of our flour and sugar coupons to make a cake, but he said he couldn't stay for dinner. We thought he was here to tell us to come back to church, but instead he said it might be best if we stayed away a bit longer. He said it would cause disruption. Oh, he was plenty nice about it, patting Ma's elbow and telling her things would be back to normal before she knew it. Thank goodness for *your* mother having that baby. It's the first thing that's distracted her."

I let out a little groan. "I'm sorry, Lou. I never meant for it to happen."

"Well, why did you have to go and tell me?" she snapped, slapping her hands against her knees. "I could have gone on pretending, telling myself there was a chance it wasn't you."

"Because I want to make things right," I said.

Lou scoffed. "By telling me you were never really my friend when a friend is the thing I need most?"

"I *am* your friend," I said. "And I came because I'm going to prove it."

"How?"

So I told her about what I had seen just moments before. About what I thought Bruce and Logan were going to do. And about the idea that had come to me as I watched them.

I told her if my plan worked, we could take some of Bruce Pittman's power away, once and for all.

Her scowl deepened the longer I spoke until she looked nothing short of thunderous.

"You'd better be right about this," she muttered when I was done explaining.

Or else, I could almost hear her thinking.

"I am, Lou," I said. "I promise. I won't let you down this time. I'll see you tonight?"

"Fine," she replied. Then, without sparing me so much as a glance, she turned and marched back through her door, slamming it behind her.

47

I left Lou's place and set off in the direction of the Widow Wagner's house, biking as fast as I could go. Winnie kept glancing at me and wagging her tail as she ran, and I wished she wouldn't look at me so happily. The way she looked at Jack.

When we had reached the hill that would lead us to the Widow Wagner's house, I wondered for the first time what had made her and her husband choose to start over here, as strangers in a strange land. Maybe they had been running from a bully, too. Maybe there had been no one to protect them, either.

Which made me think that maybe there *were* times

when running away was the right thing to do. Or the only thing to do, as it had been for the Musgraves. That sometimes it wasn't running away at all, but a way of standing up for yourself.

As we crested the hill, Winnie's ears pricked up, and she gave a sudden tug, nearly pulling me off my bike. I slammed on my brakes so I could rein her in. She was whining and straining toward the woods behind the widow's house.

I followed her gaze into the forest and felt my breath catch in my chest. They were giants, those trees, soaring into the sky with the morning sunlight illuminating everything between them. The forest looked so peaceful: the golden figure in the sunlit trees, the birds flying off into the horizon. I picked Winnie up so she wouldn't bark, and the two of us looked for a long minute, both resisting the urge to sprint into the forest. To run one last time.

Instead, I forced myself to stand there, drinking in the sight until there was nothing left to see.

When I finally reached the widow's porch, I stared numbly up at the note that had been left on the bottom step.

My heart felt like a ship taking on water as I unfolded it.

» «

Dear D,

Mrs. Wagner died in her sleep last night, and I couldn't wait any longer. Will you tell Dr. Penny? I don't want her to be alone too long. You could say you knocked on the door and there was no answer.

I'm sorry I didn't say goodbye, but it's better this way. I'll always remember you, and I hope you remember me, too, the way you would have before. I'm sorry if I let you down. Please take care of my girl. Remember, you're braver than you think.

Maybe we'll meet in Yonder one day.

48

That afternoon was one of the longest of my life.

When I got home, Dr. Penny was just coming downstairs from checking on Mama. Which was just as well, since his office was going to be my next stop.

"Fit as two fiddles," he told me, polishing his glasses on his sleeve and squinting at me. "When does your grandmother arrive?"

"Sunday," I answered.

"Good, good. I daresay you'll manage all right. I hear Hattie Maguire has been here helping? Hopefully she can pitch in until then."

"Doctor?"

He'd put his glasses back on, and behind them his

eyes had gone round and owlish once more. "I think you'd better check on the Wid—on Mrs. Wagner," I said, just as Jack had instructed. "I knocked on the door for a long time this morning, but there was no answer."

Dr. Penny studied me. "I'll do that. I can stop by before I head to the office. Thank you, Danny. Might I ask why you had cause to knock?"

"I—I saw a bird fly in through one of the windows," I lied. "I thought she ought to know."

"Right," said the doctor, though I had a strange feeling he didn't believe me. Dr. Penny, I remembered, was a member of the draft board, too, and would likely also know about Jack's disappearance. I held my breath, waiting for what he would say next. But he merely nodded to me. "Well, I'll be off then."

Mama and the baby, who still didn't have a name, had both fallen asleep by the time I went upstairs, so I took Winnie out to the dock.

Everyone was at school or work, so we didn't run into anyone on the way. That was fine by me. I needed to be alone with my thoughts for a while. I needed to untangle everything that had knotted together in my mind.

So I took my shoes off and sat at the end of the dock and looked out at the river. From far off, I heard the low howl of a train passing. I wondered if that's how Jack meant to travel, if even now he was stowed away on a train heading west to Tennessee. If the same tracks that carried the bodies of fallen soldiers home might carry him to safety.

Whether that was right or wrong, I didn't know anymore. I just knew that I would never tell a soul.

Perhaps word would get out eventually. One of the members of the draft board might tell. But I suspected they wouldn't. I suspected that the real reason Sergeant Womack and Officer Sawyer had come to school to speak with Mr. Bunch and Mr. Pittman was to ask them not to report Jack's desertion to any outside authorities. To keep it quiet and spare Mr. Bailey the shame that the Maguires had been made to feel. All because I hadn't kept Lou's secret.

But I would keep Jack's.

I would never speak of what I had seen in the forest at Mrs. Wagner's that morning. A man who had never gotten to be a boy—or maybe it was a boy who wasn't yet ready to be a man—standing beneath the trees. Empty birdcages on either side of him and the flutter of bird wings stirring the air. His face tilted toward the sun, like the boy I'd seen step out of the floodwater years ago.

Except this boy didn't look like he was waiting to be saved. He looked like a boy who had been delivered.

Like he meant to take flight into the light, too.

Jack had looked so at peace there in the safety of the trees and the warmth of the sun. I couldn't bear the thought of shattering it.

And so, I had let him go. Had said nothing as he disappeared over the dappled slope, fading away into the forest forever.

I decided in that moment that he deserved some peace after so much war.

Because there were all kinds of wars, weren't there? For years, it felt like we had all been waiting for the war to pull us in one way or another. But what if war had already come? What if there were wars—some small, others vast—happening around us all along, and we had been missing our chance to fight?

Mama had told me that Hitler turned Germans against the Jewish people little by little. Which meant that his terrible and sweeping campaign had started with small things. Like eyes that did not want to see, just as I hadn't wanted to see how much Jack was suffering. Whispers that grew into stories like the ones we told about Mrs. Wagner, that marked her out as different and dangerous. And shoulders that went cold in the turning away, the way Foggy Gap had turned their backs on the Musgraves, and then the Maguires.

Perhaps when I had asked Mama if what was happening in Germany could happen here, what I really wanted to know was what *I* would have done if it did. If I could let myself be swept up in that ruthless wave of cruelty. That was the question that had been tugging at me ever since Mama had told me about the camps.

But I finally understood that the answer to what I *would* do was in what I did now. Courage wasn't something you could save up for a rainy day. Courage took practice. Because if I didn't stand up for my best friend now, how could I hope to stand up for a neighbor, or a classmate, or a stranger when the time came? If I couldn't confront the small injustices, how could I fight the bigger ones?

I was starting to see how a little wrong made way for another little wrong, and another and another, until all those wrongs became something enormous and monstrous and wicked.

I had my answer, but it wasn't too late to change it. I might have been too young to fight in the war, but I was old enough to learn from it. And what I had learned was this: courage *always* counted. And courage started at home.

49

When the river began to ripple with golden afternoon sunlight, I called to Winnie—who was sopping wet and chewing enthusiastically at a stick on the banks nearby—and headed for home.

When I got there, Mama asked me to hold the baby while she drew herself a bath. My little sister was as awake as I had seen her, her little blue eyes open and scanning her surroundings before landing on my face.

I put a finger to her cheek. I stroked it gently, like she was something made out of clay but not hardened yet. Like if I pressed her flesh with my finger, the dent might stay.

"Hello," I murmured to her. "I'm your big brother,

Danny. Hopefully, I'll make a good brother. I'll try anyway. I'll try to be the kind of brother you'll be proud to have."

But by then, her eyes had closed again and her breath had softened. She was already fast asleep. I didn't know what to do with her, and I didn't want to wake her up, so I just held her that way until Mama reappeared sometime later and my left arm had gone all stiff.

"Look at that," she said. "You're a natural."

I had to admit, it was nice, holding her that way. Peaceful after everything the day had already brought. The rise and fall of her little chest soothed the anxiety I felt over what was still to come.

"You look very thoughtful," Mama said with a smile, sitting down next to me and gently pulling the baby onto her lap.

"I need to borrow something from the *Herald* office," I said, "and I need to go somewhere tonight."

She frowned at me. "Does this have to do with Jack?"

From my pocket, I pulled out the note Jack had left me. Half of it, at least. I had torn away the half that mentioned Mrs. Wagner.

Mama took the note, shadows tugging at the corners of her mouth as she read. "Oh, Danny," she said. There were tears shining through her eyes when she looked up. "I'm so sorry. It must have simply been too much. Living with that man. I wish he had come to us instead of leaving. I just hope he's safe."

"He is, Mama," I said.

"How do you know?" she asked, studying me closely.

"I just do."

She pointed to the bottom of the letter. "What does this mean?" she asked. "'Maybe I'll see you in Yonder one day'?"

"I don't know," I said, after a pause. It was the only honest answer I could give, because Yonder felt awfully far away just then.

"The thing I have to do . . . ," I started. "It's something he would want me to do."

Remember, you're braver than you think.

"But you aren't going to tell me what it is?"

I shook my head. I worried if I told her, she wouldn't let me.

"Not yet," I said. "Not until tomorrow. But it's what's right, Mama. I promise."

She looked from me to the baby and back again. "All right, then," she said finally. "As long as *you'll* be safe."

"I will," I said. I hoped that I was telling the truth.

"And, Mama?"

"Hmm?"

"I have an idea. About the baby's name."

50

The sun was beginning to set when I left for the *Herald* office. The sky had gone a reddish pink, the color of the apples that would ripen in our orchards in October and fill our pies through December.

Thankfully, the office was empty when I arrived. I tied Winnie to the lamppost outside. At first, I thought I should leave her back at the house. What if she gave us away? But then I had imagined me and Lou taking on Bruce and Logan and realized that we would need all the help we could get.

I used Mama's keys to get inside, then went to the closet where the cameras were kept. I eyed the press camera, but decided it was too big, and anyway, I would have to change the film after each shot, which meant I would probably only get one. Instead, I chose the smaller Contax and the flash—which would mount on top—along with a few bulbs, and put in a new roll of film. Mr. Sawyer, Officer Sawyer's father, took pictures for the paper before he'd left for war, and he'd showed me once how to operate the camera. I said a silent thank-you to him as I made my preparations.

When the camera was ready, I stowed my supplies carefully in my saddlebags, where there was just room for them, and locked the door behind me.

Shadows fell over Poplar Street as Winnie and I rode off. The shops and offices had gone dark as the house lights began to blink on like a field full of fireflies, orange and yellow and gold.

There was one last thing to do before I went to the Maguires' place. Before I'd left home, I had filled my saddlebags with the contents of my scrap-metal collection. Each time I had spotted the gleam of metal, I had swooped down on it, imagining the hero's reception I would get when I won the contest.

But I didn't want a hero's reception anymore. And besides, I knew someone who needed it much more. Under the cover of darkness, I unloaded everything I had found and carried it to the Prices' porch, where Dylan would find it the next morning. Then I set off into the night.

» «

When I arrived at the Maguires' house, I could see that Mrs. Maguire and Lou were in the kitchen, washing and drying the dinner dishes, while Mr. Maguire read on the sofa and the boys played at his feet.

I would have to wait until Mrs. Maguire herded everyone to bed, so I took my time choosing the best spot. I was sure that Bruce would paint where his message would be visible to passersby, so finally I chose a place behind a mossy boulder that gave me a view of both the front of the house and barn. I screwed the bulb into the flash and attached the flash to the camera. When that was done, Winnie laid against my lap, and I stroked her ears to keep myself calm.

One by one, the lights turned off in the Maguires' house. Thankfully, the moon was nearly full, and its glow washed over the forest like the silver ocean waves I had once splashed in with Mama. I closed my eyes, imagining myself swimming in deeper and deeper.

By the time I opened them again, cricket song surrounded me, swelling into a crescendo.

After a while, I heard a sound that didn't belong to the forest. The creak of a screen door being opened ever so slowly. In the moonlight, I saw Lou come creeping out. She stopped on the porch, her eyes scanning the darkness.

I flicked on the flashlight I had brought. Four short flashes for *H*, then one short, one long, and one short for *R*. The Morse code abbreviation for *here*.

"Turn that thing off!" Lou hissed. "Once would have been enough."

"Sorry," I muttered sheepishly. "I've just never been able to actually use Morse code before."

"It doesn't matter," she said, kneeling down next to me. "You came."

"Of course I did," I replied, a little hurt at the surprise in her voice.

"Did you bring it?"

I held up the camera, and Lou nodded. "What did you tell your mom?"

"That I needed it for a good cause."

"Are you sure it's tonight?" she asked.

"I'm sure." Bruce and Logan must have gotten up early to hide the paint in the woods so that if anyone saw them walking over tonight, they wouldn't be caught red-handed—literally. But they wouldn't want the paint to sit there any longer than it had to, and risk someone stumbling upon it.

And with that, there was nothing left to do but wait. After a while, Lou pulled out a deck of cards, and we began to play go fish. But we didn't talk much. She wasn't cold exactly, more like stiff, as she asked if I had any sevens or twos or told me to go fish. She didn't brag when she won or roll her eyes when I did.

I was starting to understand that a friendship could

be broken in a single moment, but it took much longer to put it right again. And that made a certain kind of sense. It was just like mending a waterlogged watch or a dropped dish. You had to be patient and dedicated. You had to care enough about the thing you had broken to make it worth the time it took to fix.

Finally, Winnie's ears perked up, and she pointed her nose to the woods behind us. She let out a low growl, and I searched my pockets for the jerky I had taken from the pantry earlier. A bribe to keep her quiet.

As I handed it to her, we heard the sound of feet moving softly through the ferns. Lou and I exchanged a wide-eyed glance. In another moment, two sets of legs appeared, moving through the woods a few yards away. I heard a whisper, too, but over the sound of the crickets, I couldn't make out any words.

We watched from our hiding spot as two figures broke through the trees and into the Maguires' yard. Each carried a bucket of paint in one hand and a paintbrush in the other. The taller of the two—which must have been Logan—nodded toward the side of the barn that was closest to town, which you could see from all the way down the road.

After a moment's whispered conversation, the boys set to work.

I nearly jumped from my skin as I felt something squeeze my arm before realizing it was only Lou. She looked solemn in the silver light, and I was sure I saw her lower lip give a brief tremble.

"What do you think they're going to write?" she whispered.

"I don't know," I said. "But . . . I think we have to find out. If we take the picture before they do anything, it won't be proof of much."

She nodded, then pulled Winnie's head onto her lap. Her other hand still held tightly to my arm.

I squinted through the dark to watch Bruce and Logan work. Logan painted on each letter, and then Bruce came behind, filling it in darker. It must only have taken them a few minutes, but the seconds seemed to stretch and stick like spiderwebs as we watched them spell out their message.

C —
O —
W —
A —
R —
D —
S —

N —
O —
T —

W —
E —
L —

Lou's grip tightened, her nails digging into my arm.

"That's enough," she hissed. *"Cowards not welcome here.* That's what they're writing. We don't need to let them go on with it any longer."

"All right," I said, over the noise of my banging heart. "Let's go."

Lou stood up and began to inch forward. I threw Winnie another piece of jerky so she would stay, then followed behind with the camera in hand.

There were three things that had to happen for our plan to work.

First, we couldn't give ourselves away before I had a chance to take the picture. Second, I had to take a picture of them that showed their faces clearly enough to be identifiable. And third, we had to get away before they could catch us and destroy our evidence.

I gripped the camera hard with my trembling hands as I crouched over and followed Lou past the trees and into the yard. My stomach gave a violent twist as I left our cover behind. If Bruce or Logan turned around, they would see us. *When* they turned around, I corrected myself. Not if.

There was no going back now. One way or another, Bruce and I would finally come face-to-face.

When we had crept as far as we dared, we came to a stop, and I raised the viewfinder to my eye. Then I heard Lou's sharp whistle.

Even though we had discussed this part of the plan, the noise still came as a shock. Bruce and Logan turned, just as we thought they would, but in my surprise, I hesitated a moment before taking the picture.

"Take it, Danny!" Lou cried.

Click! The flash lit up, blinding us all temporarily.

For another moment, the figures stayed frozen, like we were already looking at the picture we had taken instead of the real thing.

Then I heard a voice growl "Get that camera!"

A second later, they were barreling straight for us.

51

"*Go!*" *I whispered to* Lou, pushing the camera into her arms.

This, too, was part of the plan. Though I had more experience in running from a fight, Lou was faster. She had the better chance of getting to the door and making it inside before Bruce or Logan caught her. I would hold them off as long as I could to give her time.

Lou and I locked eyes for a second, then she took off over the grass.

At first, it seemed like both Bruce and Logan were headed for me, but then I heard the same gruff voice of a moment ago. "You stay with him. I'll go after the girl."

"Run, Lou!" I cried.

I thought it was Logan who was coming for me, but as the boy steamed forward, I realized it was Bruce. He was already pulling one arm back into a fist. Instinctively, I ducked. At the same time, I stuck one foot out in front of me and felt Bruce's shin whack into mine before his feet left the ground.

"That," I said, "was for Lou."

It seemed fitting, felling Bruce with a move I had learned from him. But I didn't have time to celebrate. I looked up to see that Logan had nearly caught Lou. As I began to run after them, he lunged forward and reached for her shoulder, only just missing. As he fell, he caught her leg, instead. Then she, too, went flying into the grass.

She screamed as she launched a kick back, the sole of her shoe hitting Logan in the head. He gave a grunt of pain. "You little—"

Lou twisted around and saw me coming. She saw, too, Logan getting to his knees, about to dive forward for the camera.

"Catch, Danny!"

The next thing I knew, the camera was spiraling through the air, and I was rushing to meet it. I fumbled to catch it, but it fell through my fingers into the grass. At least I had interrupted its fall. I prayed it hadn't broken.

"Behind you!" Lou shouted.

I turned to see Bruce back on his feet, shooting like an arrow toward me. Then he gave a sudden gasp and let out a cry. There was something holding him back. A flash of white teeth clamped around his ankle as Winnie tugged at his leg.

Logan was lifting Lou to her feet by her collar, his face a slash of rage in the dark. In a matter of seconds, I had reached into my pocket for a new flash bulb, popped the first bulb out and screwed the second in. Then I raised the camera to my eye again and snapped another picture, hoping that the flash would give Lou the second she needed to wiggle free.

The light went off, illuminating the face of her attacker. I hadn't been able to see it clearly in the first photo but now, close up, I could.

It wasn't Logan. It was Mr. Pittman.

And as he blinked, stunned by the light, Lou picked up her foot and launched it into his stomach with all the might of the feisty field pony she had always reminded me of.

As Mr. Pittman bent double, a door slammed, and a new voice rang out.

"Who the devil is out there?" came Mr. Maguire's voice from the porch. The lights in the house were blazing bright once more, though I hadn't noticed them turning on.

Bruce whimpered from behind me as I rushed to Lou's side, knocking hard into Mr. Pittman as he ran to retrieve his son. For a split second, he glared at me.

"And that," I muttered, "was for the Musgraves."

"It's me, Daddy!" Lou cried.

"Winnie, come!" I commanded.

Winnie released her grip on Bruce and ran to my side as Mr. Pittman helped Bruce to his feet.

Bruce looked at me for a second before his father pulled him away, gnashing his teeth. "You'll regret this," he spat at me.

He was wrong. I already regretted many things I had done—or hadn't—in my life, and I might come to regret many more.

But what I did that night would never be one of them.

52

Mr. and Mrs. Maguire were both devastated. It was terrible to see them that way, Mr. Maguire staring blankly at the giant words scrawled in red, Mrs. Maguire weeping into his shoulder.

"I don't understand," Mrs. Maguire said, once we were all back in the warm kitchen. "How did you know they were going to do it? And why did you let them?"

"Danny saw Bruce and Logan Abbot hiding the paint cans this morning. They already did the same thing at the Widow Wagner's house."

I held up the camera in answer to the second question. "We could have stopped the Pittmans from painting your barn," I said. "But that wouldn't be enough to stop them from doing the same thing to someone else."

"I see," Mr. Maguire said. His face looked haggard and old under the light. He had a farmer's face—one that needed sunlight and rain as much as his crops did. "You took their picture. And what do you mean to do with it?"

"Print it," I told him. "In the newspaper. So everyone can see what kind of people the Pittmans are."

I thought we would be revealing Bruce's character. I'd never dreamed that his *father* had been the one behind the graffiti. But I was coming to learn that there were great men and women in the world, and small ones, too. And Mr. Pittman, for all his farms and power and shiny cars, was as small as they came.

All the better that the whole valley knew exactly where Bruce got his meanness from.

But Mr. Maguire shook his head. "No," he said. "I don't think so. This family's already been made a spectacle. I won't give them all something else to stare at."

We all jumped as Mrs. Maguire banged her hand onto the table. "This family's lived in shame long enough," she barked. "And I won't let Nick Pittman get away with this. I won't feel ashamed of my son any longer. Lou and Danny are right. Let the *Pittmans* be ashamed. They're the cowards. Not my George."

Then she began to sob, and I decided it was time for me to go.

53

Although Mama was angry at me for staying out so late and making her worry, she softened when I told her where I had been. She also agreed that the picture of the Pittmans had to be printed. Two mornings later, they were on the front page of the *Hilltop Herald*.

After that, some things changed, and some didn't.

I was up at dawn, like every other day, to deliver the paper. Just like I would be the next day, and the next.

My route was a little shorter now that there was no one left in Mrs. Wagner's house. But most days I biked there anyway and stopped for a moment or two to think. The same edition that carried the story about the Maguires' barn had a small article about her death. It seemed no one had known much about her, because there were very few details. And, of course, there was no mention of what she had done for Jack.

In the end, she had helped him more than any of the rest of us. And he was the only one who had seen past the stories we all told about her. It seemed right that they had found one another.

It turned out I was pretty handy with a camera. And it wasn't the shot of the Pittmans painting the Maguires' barn that really got people talking. It was the one of Mr. Pittman holding Lou by her collar, the hatred finally laid bare on his face.

"That poor thing," I overheard Mrs. Hooper saying the following day, when I'd gone to the office to pick up some things for Mama. "I hate to think what Mr. Pittman might have done next."

"I always thought he had a mean streak," replied Mr. Ogletree. "But a grown man treating a little girl like that? Shame on him."

I was glad to hear the shock, the outrage people felt over that picture. But it made me sad, too. Because none of them had had the same outrage to spare the Musgraves. And Mr. Pittman had done a lot worse to them.

Bruce didn't come back to school for the last day of the year. He wasn't at the special assembly that Saturday where Dylan Price was announced as the winner of the scrap-metal contest, and where an army major presented him with his own medal. Dylan actually smiled as the school cheered for him. Mrs. Price was there in the audience applauding, too. It was the first time I had seen her leave the house since her husband was killed.

"Was it you?" Dylan had asked me that morning, in the hallway before the assembly.

I stared at him blankly. "Was what me?"

"Never mind," he said, looking puzzled but pleased.

Dylan wasn't the only hero that day. After the assembly, everyone crowded around Lou—who was waiting for me by the bike racks—to hear how she had fought off Mr. Pittman, asking if it was true that he'd really aimed a shotgun at her or that she had nearly died.

"Nah," she said, basking in all the attention. "He wasn't so tough. Tougher than Bruce, though. You should have heard the way he howled when Danny tripped him up. Like a cat in cold water."

She caught my eye through the laughing kids and smiled. I smiled back and nodded to the school steps, where Logan stood alone, with only his own scowl for company.

I couldn't imagine anyone laughing like that at Bruce a week ago. But it was like an enchantment had been broken, and no one was afraid anymore. I only wished it hadn't taken us so long.

» «

The Pittmans weren't in church that Sunday, either. Word was that Mr. Pittman had been called out of state on a mysterious emergency. He had taken his family with him to spend the summer in Maryland, though not before resigning his place on the draft board.

"Probably hoping folks will forget by the time he comes back," Mama said. "But I think he'll be in for a nasty surprise. These mountains have long memories."

The Pittmans' pew didn't sit empty, though. That Sunday, Mrs. Maguire entered the church just before the service started and marched down the aisle with her chin held high, one of her boys on each side. Then came Mr. Maguire, his hair slicked back and his eyes downcast. And finally, Lou, who had somehow been wrangled into a pink checkered dress with a bow at the waist. She looked like she might have saved one last kick to the stomach for the first person who told her how darling she looked.

Pastor Douglass read from the Gospel of John that morning. "Let he who is without sin be the first to judge," he reminded his congregation. But he needn't have bothered.

If people had changed their minds about the Pittmans, then they'd had a change of *heart* when it came to the Maguires. Suddenly it seemed everyone agreed that "some people" had been treating them unfairly, and that they had been through enough already.

(Though no one seemed to agree on just who "some people" were.)

"Poor George *did* enlist after all," muttered Mrs. Dinwiddie in the pew in front of me, Mama, and the baby. "He went by choice."

"I always did like him," Mrs. Updike replied. "You know, he used to come and slop the pigs for me when my Alfie was bedridden. Wouldn't even let me pay him with a pie. But war can do funny things to a body. Anyone might have done what he did, really."

After the service that Sunday, the line to shake the Maguires' hands was longer than the line to shake Pastor Douglass's.

Once folks were done speaking to the Maguires, many of them wandered over to Mama, eager to see the new baby.

"Well, isn't she a doll," Mrs. Ballentine cooed. "What's her name?"

Mama and I shared a look.

"Daphne," Mama said. "Her name is Daphne."

"After Mrs. Musgrave," I added.

The librarian's face froze, and a blush climbed into her cheeks. I saw Mrs. Dinwiddie and Mrs. Updike exchange uncertain looks.

"How beautiful," said Mrs. Pattershaw, who had come up behind me without my noticing. She shot me a little smile.

Daphne Musgrave might have been forced to leave Foggy Gap, but Daphne Timmons would live there for many years to come, a reminder of her namesake. One nobody could look away from.

It was just a name, I knew. Not enough. Not a magic spell to change the past or the future. But when they saw my little sister and spoke her name, I hoped the people of Foggy Gap would see themselves, too, prejudices and all. I hoped Daphne would make *them* want to be better, just as she made me want to be.

Daphne was a new beginning—and *just* the beginning.

Lou caught my eye from over her mother's shoulder and nodded toward the graveyard.

"I'll be right back," I said to Mama.

I joined Lou, and together we walked around the far side of the church to the graveyard where our friendship had begun, and where it had nearly ended. It was the first Sunday of summer, and it felt like it. I rolled up my shirtsleeves as Lou untied the bow around her waist and crumpled it inside one fist.

She sank down into the long grass and slumped back against a lichen-dappled tombstone, as casually as if it were her own sofa.

"Well," she said, peering at me as I sat down beside her.

"Well," I echoed hesitantly.

"I hear the Pittmans won't be showing their faces around here for a while," she said. Then she broke into a toothy smile.

"Too bad," I said. "There's at least a dozen ladies in that church who would have loved to take a whack at Mr. Pittman before he ran off."

Lou giggled, and a warm, comfortable moment of silence stretched between us, like a shared blanket around our shoulders.

"I always knew Bruce was a coward deep down," Lou said, plucking a blade of grass and holding it up to the sun. "And I knew Mr. Pittman wasn't any summer peach. But I didn't know he was as bad as Bruce. *Worse*, even."

"I did," I replied quietly.

"I wonder if Bruce ever had a choice," Lou wondered aloud. "With a father like that, maybe he was always going to be a bully."

"Jack wasn't a bully," I said.

"No, I guess not." Lou looked over at me, and her eyes softened in the sun. "I'm sorry we couldn't find him, Danny. I know he was a good friend to you."

At the assembly the day before, I had shown Lou the same half of Jack's note I had shown Mama. She seemed disappointed that there wasn't a big cover-up to expose but said that it just went to show that the simplest solution is usually the right one.

"It's okay," I said, though it wasn't, not really. "I'm sorry I wasn't a better friend to *you*."

Lou shrugged, but her eyes had sharpened once more, the light in them like the silver glint of twin shields.

Just then, I heard Mama calling.

"I have to go," I told Lou. "We have to meet Granny Mabel's train."

Lou nodded, but stayed where she was as I stood. "Wait."

"Yeah?"

"I forgive you, Danny," she said. "But if you ever do anything like that again, you'll get worse than Mr. Pittman got."

I grinned. "Deal," I said.

I hesitated over a patch of Queen Anne's lace, then plucked one of the flowers and walked to the corner of the graveyard, where Sarah Bailey rested. The feather Jack put there had blown away. I laid the flower in its place.

Mama called my name again, and I turned to go.

Though I was in a graveyard, for once I felt free of ghosts. I broke into a run, and for the first time, it felt like I wasn't running away.

54

After

It was sometime later that summer that I heard through Mama, who heard through Mrs. Dinwiddie, that John Bailey had died in his sleep one night. He was buried next to his wife in the churchyard.

The news got me thinking again about the war medal Lou and I had found in the Baileys' cabin. What, I wondered, had happened to it?

I would never know exactly how Mr. Bailey came to be the man who gave Jack black eyes and broken ribs. But I knew courage in a war couldn't make up for the things he had done to his son. Just like it was wrong to brand George Maguire a coward for one moment of fear, I couldn't think of Mr. Bailey as a hero just because he'd been brave in battle. Courage was important, but it wasn't much without conscience.

Of course, it was possible that Jack was right, and the war really had changed his father in ways beyond his control. But no matter what, it had been up to the rest of us in Foggy Gap to stop Mr. Bailey. To be the family to Jack that his own father couldn't be. It might have been his fists that had done the damage, but we all had a hand in what Jack had been made to suffer.

Some folks might have said Jack's decision to leave made him a coward, but I had my doubts about that. Jack had always looked out for anyone who needed helping, even a stranger like I had once been to him. If we had paid him back in kind, everything might have turned out differently. And if there were more people like Jack around, there might have been no war to begin with.

I turned these thoughts over and over in my head as summer slowly gave way to autumn, crimson and caramel creeping into the trees. And I wondered sometimes if the war would follow Daddy home, too. If we would find him changed.

But when he returned that October, he was just the same as he'd always been, though the shrapnel wound in his leg meant that he would never be able to move as he had before. He would walk through the world a little slower, a little heavier.

That didn't stop him, though, from throwing Daphne up in the air whenever he saw her, making her squeal with joy, which in turn made the rest of us laugh.

And after the war ended a year and a half later, we heard from the Musgraves that Mr. Musgrave had returned safe and sound, too. But he had been there at the liberation of Dachau, one of the camps Mama had told me about, which we came to call concentration camps. And the memory of it, Mrs. Musgrave wrote, would never leave him: the people who had clung to life against all the odds, and the ones who hadn't been able to any longer.

When the photos of the camps were published, suddenly everyone was talking about it, just the way they had done after the photos of the Pittmans had been printed in the *Hilltop Herald*.

They were aghast, disbelieving. *How could this have happened? Why didn't anybody stop it?*

But I knew. Because we had all stood by, too. And that was how terrible wrongs began.

As Daphne grew older, I began taking her and Winnie for walks in the forest, where I would point out the red oaks with the acorns turkeys liked best, and the sycamore with the hollow big enough for a bear den, and the best rocks to find crawdaddies underneath. I often brought one of the *Herald's* cameras with me, to take pictures of the light dancing through the oak leaves or snow falling into the river. I liked the way the camera could reveal things the eye couldn't see on its own. I had decided I wanted to be a photojournalist one day, to keep using pictures to help people see what had been invisible to them before.

I felt Jack with me in those woods, too, blowing through the trees on the wind. Laughing along with the gurgling creeks. I heard his voice all the time. *Remember, you're braver than you think.*

Sometimes, images of Yonder still came to me deep in the night.

In my dreams, the log cabins in the town were both humble and proud, their windows thrown open wide in invitation. The smell of the forest—white pine and rain on moss—blew into the houses, and the smell of baking—fresh blackberries and melting butter— wafted out of them.

Children ran barefoot through the streets and trees, chasing each other and gasping with laughter. Fiddle music came from somewhere nearby. Shadows raced overhead, and I looked up to see the birds Jack had told me about—the jewelbirds—crisscrossing through the sky like brightly colored kites cut loose from their strings.

Jack was there sometimes, always a boy and never a man, eating at the mile-long table or running with the other children. His eyes were green with the peace of the forest.

But I understood by then that Yonder had never been more than just that—a wonderful dream. A hope whispered to a small, scared boy on dark nights.

There was no place on earth where the people had never heard of war and never fought. Not on this side of the grave, anyway. Yonder was like the horizon, a place you could never quite reach.

But though we might never reach it, we could at least come closer. It was like Mama said. Yonder was a *direction*. One we could all follow. If we couldn't find a place with no evil, at least we could find ourselves in one where people had the courage to stand up to it.

I liked to think, though, that there was a real town out there somewhere, tucked deep away in the hills, slowly crumbling and deserted but for the flocks of jewelbirds who filled the sky with color and the air with song. Who loved fiercely and flew freely without fear of being shot.

Who lived, truly, in peace.

Acknowledgments

Thanks is due first and foremost to the ever amazing editorial team at HarperCollins—Alyson Day, Megan Ilnitzki, and Eva Lynch-Comer—for giving my words a home, believing in this story, and shaping it into the novel it has become. I'm grateful to be a part of the larger Harper Team, including Vincent Cusenza, Jon Howard, Aubrey Churchward, Lena Reilly, Emma Meyer, and James Neel.

Thanks also to illustrator Leo Nickolls and designer Laura Mock, who must be actual alchemists to have distilled this story into such a stunning cover.

To my inimitable agent, Sarah Davies, who I will miss dearly but wish all the best in retirement, and to the wonderful Chelsea Eberly for taking the wheel—I can't wait to see where the road takes us!

To my many early readers, each of whom provided me with valuable insights on different characters, sections, and drafts of this story: Becca AbuRakia-Einhorn,

Shelley Crisp, Kristin Gray, Leah Henderson, Supriya Kelkar, Susanna Klingenberg, Nicole Overton, Nancy Ruth Patterson, Paul Ringel, Carlie Sorosiak, and Sara Stohler. And to my fellow Writer's Cramp members, who cheered me on chapter by chapter, particularly York Wilson for his expertise on antique cameras.

To Karina Yan Glaser, Alan Gratz, and Tae Keller for their incredibly kind words about this story.

To Jim Crisp, Bob Erwin, Betty McCullough, and Sara Stohler (whose own mother, Pearl, is echoed in Danny's mama) for sharing your memories of the war years with me—some painful, some humorous, all informative. You opened a window for me into the 1940s without which I could not have imagined this book. Thank you for allowing me to enrich Danny's story with bits of your own.

There were many other sources I relied upon in my research—too many to list them all here—but I will mention those that I turned to the most. I am grateful to the US Holocaust Museum's History Unfolded database, the *Watauga Democrat* for sharing their archives with me, and the following titles for making the war years come alive: *World War II on the Air: Edward R. Murrow and the Broadcasts That Riveted a Nation* by Mark Bernstein and Alex Lubertozzi; *The American Home Front 1941–1942* by Alistair Cooke; *No Ordinary Time: Franklin & Eleanor Roosevelt: The Home*

Front in World War II by Doris Kearns Goodwin; and *Buried by the Times: The Holocaust and America's Most Important Newspaper* by Laurel Leff.

Finally, I'm indebted to Nikole Hannah-Jones's two-part investigation into the historical dispossession of Black landowners and farmers, "The Land of Our Fathers" (part of the 1619 podcast series), which helped make it possible for me to craft the Musgraves' story.

Last, I am forever indebted to my family and friends for their support and guidance. You know who you are, and you know that I love you. I owe a special thanks to Chloe Lemaire, who watched over my infant son early in the pandemic, which allowed me to write this book. Childcare workers and educators make our world go round, and we would be lost without them.

Author's Note

This book takes place in the 1940s, when there was far less support available for children experiencing neglect and abuse. Fortunately, that support does exist today. Every child deserves to feel safe in their home, and that means **you**! If you don't feel safe, *please* reach out to get help. Talk to a trusted adult outside your home, like a teacher or counselor, or call the Childhelp National Child Abuse Hotline at 1-800-4-A-CHILD (1-800-422-4453). And, of course, in an emergency, always call 911.

Oftentimes, it can be difficult or scary for someone being abused to get help themselves. So if you suspect a friend might be in an abusive situation, help them by reaching out to an adult you trust and letting your friend know you are there for them no matter what.

Historical Notes

Though lots has been written about Europe during World War II, not many books have focused on the American home front. These days, most of us don't know very much about what was going on in the US during the war years, even though Americans' lives were hugely impacted by the war. Almost all those who stayed behind knew someone who had enlisted or been drafted, and many at home found ways big and small to contribute to the war effort.

In some senses, World War II was America at its best. Overseas, Americans, along with our allies, fought bravely for the values of democracy. Over 400,000 Americans lost their lives in the war, and we are still indebted to them today. At home, Americans were unified in working hard and sacrificing for the good of the nation. That's why so many of us think of America as the good guys—the heroes—of the war.

But, as Danny learns, there is usually more to a

hero than meets the eye, and the truth of America's role in World War II is more complicated. Just like it's important to celebrate the ways we contributed to a more just world, we also need to learn from the opportunities we missed to create a more just country.

First, it is commonly thought that Americans did not know about Hitler's Jewish extermination campaign until after concentration camps were discovered and liberated. But it was clear to both the Roosevelt administration and the American public that German Jews were imperiled long before the war began, as they faced increasing persecution and violence. Still, President Roosevelt resisted calls to allow more German refugees into the United States, even turning away a ship of nearly a thousand Jewish refugees who sought asylum in 1939. Many of those passengers would later be interned in concentration camps and killed at the hands of the Nazis.

By 1942, the details of Hitler's campaign had been made public. The famous war journalist Edward R. Murrow announced in his December 13 broadcast that "millions of human beings, most of them Jews, are being gathered up with ruthless efficiency and murdered." While a few media outlets, like *The Nation* and *The New Republic*, tried to raise the alarm about the terrible events happening overseas—and rally support for intervention—most gave little page space to covering the genocide.

But the articles *were* there. The United States Holocaust Memorial Museum has compiled a searchable database, History Unfolded, which contains thousands of articles that were written and reprinted across the US about Hitler's extermination campaign, the Warsaw Ghetto Uprising, and many other events pertaining to the Holocaust. The headlines and articles mentioned in this book are all based on articles from the database.

One startling but typical example I came across in my research was an article from the *Watauga Democrat* headlined: "2,000,000 Jews Are Slain by the Axis." The article was only one paragraph long, on page eight, and above the prices of meat. It was printed on Christmas Eve, 1942. How, I wondered, could anyone think that the loss of millions of lives was no more newsworthy than meat prices? Who could read the first article, then simply go on to read the next?

So while some Americans genuinely may not have known anything about the unfolding tragedy, most would have held some of that knowledge in the back of their minds. Had Americans united around helping European Jews in the way they united around the war effort, President Roosevelt might have felt pressure to prioritize rescuing some of those who were murdered.

Second, while the US used World War II as an opportunity to protect and spread democracy overseas, the same cannot be said for democratic rights at home. Thousands of Japanese Americans were rounded up and sent to internment camps, many permanently losing their jobs, homes, and land in the process—even those who would go on to fight in the war. Meanwhile, many Black men and women, like Mr. Musgrave, were eager to do their part but were not allowed to enlist because of their race. Doris Miller, the hero mentioned in Mrs. Musgrave's letter, had been allowed to enlist in the navy but only as a messman who cooked, served, and cleaned for the other sailors. That did not stop him from manning an antiaircraft machine gun and saving wounded shipmates, including his own captain, during the Japanese attack on Pearl Harbor.

When, later in the war, Black men and women were allowed to enlist in larger numbers—more than 1.2 million served—they fought in segregated units and were treated as second-class citizens. Meanwhile on the home front, the Double V campaign was launched by the *Pittsburgh Courier*—the most widely read Black newspaper in the US at the time. The *Courier* urged Black Americans to do their part to conquer tyranny overseas but also to fight for their rights at home. This campaign would help lay the ground for the Civil Rights movement of the 1960s.

Unfortunately, many white Americans were unwilling to see the parallels between the Nazi persecution of Jews and the oppression of Black people and other minority groups at home. Hitler, on the other hand, had made this connection long before the war. When drafting the laws that would take rights away from Jewish people and ultimately lead to the Holocaust, the Nazi party took direct inspiration from the Jim Crow laws of the American South, and the citizenship laws that prevented American Indians and other groups from becoming US citizens.

The Musgraves are a fictional family, but their plight is one that many real Black families have experienced. Denying farm loans is just one of many ways that Black people have been unfairly treated by institutions in the US. And while Appalachia is a region people often think of as being exclusively white, it has long been home to many Black communities. For instance, the neighborhood that Mrs. Musgrave calls "the Hill" is a real place in the town of Boone, now known as Junaluska. After the Civil War, when enslaved people were finally freed and had to be paid for their work, they were often compensated in the form of land, just as Mr. Musgrave's grandfather was. But often, this land was poor quality and difficult to farm.

America and its allies won World War II, yet as a country, we didn't live up to all the values we fought for. It's important to recognize and learn from our failures as well as our triumphs, because our work is not done. We can honor the sacrifices of those who died in battle by continuing to strive for true equality and democracy. The fight goes on.

Discussion Questions

1. Mama tells Danny that "most of us have a voice, somewhere deep inside us, that tells us when we've done wrong." Can you think of a time when you had such a voice in your head? What did you do about it? What could you have done differently?

2. Danny tells us that not all stories have heroes. Is there a true hero in *Yonder?* Why or why not?

3. In what ways does *Yonder* show Americans coming together for a common purpose? What lessons can we learn from their unity?

4. How were the Musgraves treated differently from other families in Foggy Gap? Why do you think no one questioned the way they were treated?

5. The Musgraves leave Foggy Gap after they are denied a farm loan. How did this affect their

family? How might this act impact future generations of Musgraves?

6. What could Danny and his family have done differently to help Jack? What would you do if you had a friend in Jack's situation?

7. Do you agree with Jack's decision to leave Foggy Gap and Danny's decision to let him go? Why or why not?

8. In the book, Danny says: "I was starting to see how a little wrong made way for another little wrong, and another and another, until all those wrongs became something enormous and monstrous and wicked." What do you think he means by this?

9. What do you think it means to have courage *and* conscience? Why is it important to have both?

10. Visit www.newspapers.ushmm.org and search the database for newspaper articles in your community that covered the treatment of Jewish people in Europe during World War II. What do you notice about how the information is presented? What surprises you? How does coverage of the Holocaust compare to the way foreign crises are portrayed today?